LADY GRACE

MYSTERIES

KEENE PUBLIC LIBRARY
60 Winter Street
Keene, NH 03431
352-0157

KEENE PUBLIC LIBRARY
60 Winter Street
Keene, NH 03431
(603) 352-0157
www.keenepubliclibrary.org

Also available in

The Lady Grace Mysteries series

ASSASSIN

BETRAYAL

CONSPIRACY

DECEPTION

EXILE

FEUD

GOLD

HAUNTED

THE
LADY GRACE
MYSTERIES

INTRIGUE

Grace Cavendish

Jan Burchett and Sara Vogler are writing as Grave Cavendish

RED FOX

j LADY GRACE

THE LADY GRACE MYSTERIES: INTRIGUE
A RED FOX BOOK 978 1 862 30418 5

First published in Great Britain by Red Fox,
an imprint of Random House Children's Books
A Random House Group Company

This edition published 2008

1 3 5 7 9 10 8 6 4 2

Series created by Working Partners Ltd
Copyright © Working Partners Ltd, 2008
Cover illustration by David Wyatt

All rights reserved. No part of this publication may be reproduced, stored in a
retrieval system, or transmitted in any form or by any means, electronic, mechanical,
photocopying, recording or otherwise, without the prior permission of the publishers.

The Random House Group Limited makes every effort to ensure that the papers
used in its books are made from trees that have been legally sourced from well-managed
and credibly certified forests. Our paper procurement policy can be found at:
www.randomhouse.co.uk/paper.htm

Mixed Sources
Product group from well-managed
forests and other controlled sources
www.fsc.org Cert no. TT-COC-2139
© 1996 Forest Stewardship Council
FSC

Set in Bembo

Red Fox Books are published by Random House Children's Books,
61–63 Uxbridge Road, London W5 5SA

www.**kids**at**randomhouse**.co.uk
www.**rbooks**.co.uk

Addresses for companies within The Random House Group Limited can be found at: www.
randomhouse.co.uk/offices.htm

A CIP catalogue record for this book is available from the British Library.

Printed in the UK by CPI Bookmarque, Croydon, CR0 4TD

For Eileen and Alan Barnes,
with thanks for all the wonderful
holidays, and all the ones to come.

For Mine Eyes Only

The most secrete Daybooke
of my Lady Grace Cavendish,
Maid of Honour to Her Gracious Majesty
Queen Elizabeth I of that name

At Her Majesty's Palace of
Whitehall, Westminster

The Eleventh Day of August, in the Year of Our Lord 1570

In my bedchamber, early afternoon

I have a new daybooke. And I have something exciting to write in it. We are going to Southwark to see a play this very afternoon! The whole Court is in a rush to be ready, for we must leave within the hour. Mrs Champernowne, the Mistress of the Maids, has us all in a tizzy. Carmina Willoughby and Lady Jane Coningsby have scuttled to their bedchamber to change, and here in our chamber, Mary Shelton is choosing a hat to wear and the ever-so-modest Lady Sarah Bartelmy is flapping about which sleeves will best compliment her 'beautiful copper locks'.

Faith! I hope she does not look over my shoulder and see what I have written about her.

A few moments later

I stopped writing and announced that I am
thinking of putting down prayers for special use
before bedtime. Now no one will bother to look
over my shoulder. In any case, Lady Sarah usually
dismisses my writing as silly scribbling. If she only
knew some of the adventures I have recorded in
my daybookes!

I am trying not to fidget with excitement about
the play we are going to see. I have watched plays
before, but always at Court and never at an inn,
which is where most people see them. Today we go
to the inn where the players are performing
because Her Majesty is all impatience to see the
play and will not wait for them to come to the
palace and set everything up here. I think this play
will have us all on the edge of our seats, for it deals
with a murder. I can hardly wait!

I am sitting having my hair styled – by Ellie
Bunting. I still cannot get used to the idea that my
dear friend Ellie is now my tiring woman. I am
more grateful than I can say that Her Majesty gave
Ellie her new position last month and saved her
from the drudgery of the laundry. It was no more
than Ellie deserved for being most brave in helping
to solve a mystery that had upset the whole Court.

I know Ellie is very happy too – especially as she has escaped the dreadful Mrs Fadget, deputy laundress and scourge of her life. It has only been a matter of weeks but already Ellie is less skinny now that she has enough food. She looks very fine today in my old blue kirtle. It is a relief that I can now give her clothes and no one will accuse her of stealing them.

Hell's teeth! Ellie has just mistaken my scalp for a pincushion! Luckily I only cried 'Ouch!' and nothing worse. There are some trials to having such a diligent tiring woman – although I must say that Ellie has taken to her new duties like a duck to water and wastes no time in getting me dressed. Today she chose my green gown with the ivy-leaf aiglets and said she knew just how she would adorn my hair. Ellie has developed a love of fashion. She takes more time over how I look than I would myself. She is forever talking to the other tiring women and committing to memory all that they tell her. Then she improves upon their ideas. At least, she tells me they are improvements.

Last week she insisted upon trying to lighten my hair with a solution of lemon juice and lime wash. I could not see any difference in the colour of my mousy brown tresses, yet they did seem softer. And she never complains about my hair being shorter

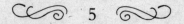

than it should. I suppose she would not dare. She was the one who cut it, after all! But it was all upon Her Majesty's service last year, when I had to be *incognito* and dress as a boy.

Faith, I have done many strange things since I took on the secret role of Her Majesty's Lady Pursuivant, seeking out all those who would trouble the Queen's peace. But I am going off the point again! Back to my news of the play – which is very exciting.

We first heard of it at the noontide meal not long since. Our goblets had just been refilled when Lady Ann Courtenay said the words that made me nearly jump off my chair with excitement.

'Has Your Majesty heard of the play that is to be performed at Southwark?'

'I have not, Lady Ann,' said the Queen, looking interested. 'What can you tell me of it?'

'The play has been performed in Kent and has now come to the Key Inn,' Lady Ann informed Her Majesty eagerly. 'It seems that the troupe are erecting a stage in the inn courtyard, and plan to put on their first performance this very afternoon. It is said to be a most unusual and fascinating play, but that is all I know.'

The Queen gave a laugh. 'I hope the good people of Southwark are better informed on the

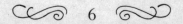

subject than you, my lady,' she said. 'Else no one will be interested enough to see this new play!'

I felt quite cross with Lady Ann for not knowing more, even though it was not really her fault. I had been hoping that a vivid description of the play would make the Queen want to see it without delay.

But Lord Robert, the Earl of Leicester, unknowingly came to my rescue. He leaned forward to Her Majesty, in that private way he has, just as if the two of them were alone. 'The play is called *Intrigue*,' he murmured, 'and is reported to have a stunning death scene at the end.'

There was a hubbub round the table at this and I wanted to shout, 'Please, please say we can go and see it, Your Majesty!' Of course, Lady Sarah and Lady Jane pretended to be unnerved by the mention of the word 'death' so that they could lean upon their gentleman neighbours and flutter their eyelashes at them. Jane and Sarah are the most competitive ladies at Court when it comes to men's attentions.

Lady Margaret Mortimer, who up till now has been one of the quietest Ladies-in-Waiting I have ever known, put down her goblet with a clatter. 'My Lord Robert!' she exclaimed. 'Is this not the play that sets up a puzzle for the audience?'

And then Lord Robert forgot his usual haughtiness and smiled. 'Yes, indeed. The play is well named, for it does sound intriguing. One of the characters is mysteriously killed and there is a prize for anyone who can guess the identity of the murderer.'

This sounded better and better! I love a good mystery, but the Queen was still unconvinced.

'But word will surely have been passed round by now,' she said, 'and many people will know the answer!'

'It seems not, My Liege,' replied Lord Robert. 'No one has managed to work the puzzle out yet. And, just to be sure, the audience is sworn to secrecy at the end of every performance.'

Now at last I saw a sparkle in the Queen's eyes. 'How interesting!' she said. 'Why did nobody tell me? I can never resist a puzzle.' She paused, frowning in concentration. Then, 'We shall see this play!' she announced. 'We shall all go to the Key Inn this very afternoon!'

There is only one thing that worries me now: I fear Her Majesty might change her mind – she is famous for doing that. Immediately Mrs Champernowne got into such a fluster.

'We have little time for the Maids to be

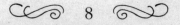

ready, My Liege,' she fretted.

'They will have as long as I,' said the Queen pointedly. 'And I will not be tardy.'

I breathed a sigh of relief. I knew I could be ready in time. But then Her Majesty's faithful councillor, Mr Secretary Cecil, put his oar in and began to deliver a veritable sermon on the evils of the village of Southwark.

'You will be venturing into a most unsavoury place, filled with all manner of low life and filth, Your Majesty,' he intoned. Ladies Jane and Sarah seized this opportunity to gasp and look frightened as he then expounded at length on the horrors of Southwark. Unfortunately he did not give any details. I bent towards Mary Shelton; she always knows everything.

'What horrors does he mean?' I whispered.

'I'll warrant he is thinking of the many gambling and drinking dens,' she whispered back.

'Oh.' I nodded.

'And the bull and bear-baiting rings that excite more gambling and drinking among the common folk!'

I shuddered; I hate seeing animals injured or killed for sport.

'And, of course, with all that gambling and drinking, the folk are fair prey to having their

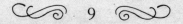

purses cut and stolen,' Mary told me. 'It is a paradise for thieves, by all accounts.'

'Oh, dear!' I murmured. But I was thinking that all this would be exciting to see – from the safety of the Queen's entourage, of course.

'I pray you reconsider, Your Majesty,' Secretary Cecil was saying. 'The players can be summoned here to Court to perform in a few days time.'

'Dear Mr Cecil,' said the Queen when he had finished, 'your concern for my wellbeing does you credit, but I would see this play without delay.'

I could have leaped from my seat and hugged her, but no one is allowed to do that to the Queen.

Secretary Cecil bowed his head and turned to Mr Hatton, the Captain of the Gentlemen of the Guard. 'We must send men to prepare,' he said. Mr Hatton nodded.

Ellie has just picked up a handful of trinkets which she is now weaving into my hair. She is determined to be the best tiring woman ever. I think she feels she owes it to Her Majesty for the trust the Queen has placed in her.

A funny thing happened just now. Olwen was lacing on Lady Sarah's wrist ruffs when Sarah exclaimed, 'I am so looking forward to this play!' and raised her hand dramatically to her brow as if she were on the stage herself. Poor Olwen was pulled forward so violently that she fell on top of her mistress!

'And to think,' added Mary Shelton, once everyone was on their feet again, 'if we were still on progress, as we should have been, we would have missed it altogether!'

Mary is right. It is unusual for us to be in London in August. Her Majesty likes to spend the summer months travelling her realm, and it gives the servants back in London the chance to clean the royal palaces. Only last week we were at my lord of Leicester's home at Kenilworth Castle. We then journeyed back south, staying at various noble houses on the way. We should now be in Kent — at Knole Hall, where Her Majesty's cousin, Thomas Sackville, has the lease — but there was talk of the sweating sickness in nearby Sevenoaks so the Queen refused to go. Luckily Whitehall has been cleaned and there has been no sign of plague in London itself, so here we are.

Just then, Lady Jane and Carmina burst into our chamber. Lady Jane came straight over to see what Ellie was doing.

'Look, everyone!' she shrieked like a parrot. 'See all the time and trouble Grace is taking with her appearance. She must already have heard the news,

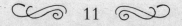

or she would not be beautifying herself so.'

'What news?' demanded Lady Sarah.

'Do you not know?' Jane began. 'In faith, we have just heard from Samuel Twyer the guard that—'

'Richard Fitzgrey is to play the main character!' Carmina interrupted excitedly, earning herself a black look from Lady Jane.

I felt Ellie's hands tighten on my hair. We had all met Richard Fitzgrey before – we'd seen him act at the Palace of Nonsuch – and I knew well that this news would set hearts and eyelashes fluttering. My new tiring woman in particular has been under Richard's spell ever since she first laid eyes on him. She has a miniature portrait of him that she carries everywhere. Indeed, of all the ladies at Court, I seem to be the only one immune to the charms of Richard Fitzgrey, but Lady Jane was determined to prove otherwise.

'Is he not the most handsome man you have ever seen, Grace?' she squawked.

What was I to say? If I said his looks were not to my taste, the other Maids would have deafened me with their shrieks of protest. As it happened, I pondered too long.

'As I thought,' smirked Jane. 'Our young Grace is lost in admiration of him!' And with that, she and Carmina rushed out of the bedchamber again.

Once they had gone, Ellie asked me to inspect my hair. I held up the glass to see her work. She had left the back down, as is the fashion, but some tresses were pinned up and adorned with trinkets and pearls. Unfortunately, one side bulged out a little like a pumpkin. Ellie could see from my face that I was not entirely delighted. She stood behind me and frowned at my reflection.

'Thank you, Ellie,' I said. 'The trinkets are very pretty. Er, but do you think it is a little lopsided?' I added, trying not to laugh. I did not want to hurt my friend's feelings – nor did I want to be whacked with a comb!

'Hmph,' Ellie snorted, her cheeks going pink. 'Your ladyship should've kept still instead of messing about with that book of yours. Then it would have been perfect.'

She began to rearrange my hair. I held up the glass and I could see that she was upset. It was even worse as Lady Sarah and Mary Shelton were now ready. I poked my tongue out at Ellie's reflection, and she managed a faint smile.

'Grace has gone woodwild, Mary!' exclaimed Sarah. 'She is pulling faces at herself.'

I heard Ellie chuckle behind me. She was laughing at me but I was glad she had cheered up.

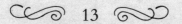 13

'You mistake me, Sarah,' I said solemnly. 'I have heard that the dreadful spotted-tongue fever has come to London and I was making sure I had not caught it.'

Ellie turned a guffaw into a loud cough as Lady Sarah stuck out her tongue to inspect it for spots. At that moment the door opened and Mrs Champernowne bustled in like a clucking hen.

'Come, come,' tutted the Mistress of the Maids. 'This will never do. Lady Sarah, put away your tongue. Have you become a simpleton? And Grace, still not ready? Put away your book. Everyone is waiting!' She held up a warning finger. 'No excuses, look you!' And then she bustled out of the room again, chivvying Lady Sarah and Mary Shelton ahead of her.

And now Ellie has put the last comb in my hair, placed my hat carefully on the top and hurried out of the chamber, doing a perfect imitation of Mrs Champernowne's bum swinging from side to side as she goes. I must needs stop writing and go . . .

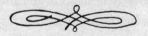

In my bedchamber, about five of the clock

We are back from Southwark, and I am finding it

hard to write as my hand is trembling. Something awful happened at the Key Inn. It has put the whole Court into uproar and— But I am jumping to the end of my tale.

Once ready, we all followed the Queen in a great noisy crowd to Privy Bridge, the landing stage where we would board our boats to cross the Thames to Southwark. Her Majesty looked magnificent. She wore a fine black gown with a most unusual partlet, gathered to fit under a small jewel-encrusted ruff. She had strings of pearls around her neck and a ring hung on a cord. I believe we will see many rings worn this way by the end of the day. One or two people were still hastily adjusting sleeves and hats. The Queen had had a lot of help to be ready in such a short time but many had not!

Ellie followed me all the way. I could feel her eyes burning into the back of my hair. I think she was willing it to stay in place. She would have swum alongside our boat if she could.

'I promise to tell you all about it when I return,' I whispered to her. Poor Ellie. Tiring women do not accompany their mistresses with the rest of the Court.

'You'd better, Grace,' Ellie replied. 'And be sure you remember every detail of Richard's looks.' She scurried off, but not before I saw her dip her hand into her pocket and pull out the little portrait of Mr Fitzgrey.

It seemed that the whole Court intended to go and see the play. I was sure some would be disappointed. I did not think an inn could possibly hold so many people. In fact, I thought that after the Queen, her ministers, her Ladies-in-Waiting, her Maids of Honour and the Gentlemen of the Guard had been accounted for, we would probably fill the inn. I wondered if there would be a fight amongst the rest of the courtiers for the last few places!

Someone jostled me. I turned to see my friend Masou's cheeky face before he swept down in a deep bow. Not that I should call him my friend – in front of others at least. I wish I did not have to make a secret of my friendship with Ellie and Masou. I do not see why a Maid of Honour cannot be friendly with those who are lowly born. If I were Queen, I would make a law about it. Hell's teeth! I hope it is not treason to write that. Besides, I could not imagine me, or anyone else, taking the place of Her Majesty.

'Forgive me, dear lady, for my clumsiness!' Masou gushed melodramatically. 'I trust I have not harmed you.'

We moved aside to the quay wall and pretended to watch the river to hide our conversation.

'Are you hoping to learn some new tricks from the players, Master Masou?' I asked innocently.

'No indeed, my Lady Grace,' he said with a wink. 'They will be coming to *me* for advice, for am I not the best tumbler at Court?'

Masou always makes this boast, but of course he is right. He performs the best acrobatics in Mr Somers's troupe. He learned how to do it as soon as he could walk, and he was not in want of employment when he and his father travelled from their home in North Africa to come to England. Like Ellie, Masou was rewarded for his bravery at Medenham Manor last month. He is now one of Her Majesty's Court Fools, with a goodly salary and a livery of red and black velvet.

'I am surprised you can tumble at all,' I whispered, 'with such a big head!'

'I thank you, my lady, for the compliment,' Masou replied, laughing. 'I have already been to the Key Inn this morning,' he went on. 'I met my good friend Richard and watched him rehearse.'

'Good friend!' I snorted. 'I recall that you called him a "clay-brained coxcomb" not so long ago, yet now you and he are like brothers! Alack, with such a new friend you will soon forget Ellie and me.'

'Fear not,' replied Masou. 'I could never forget a lady and her tiring woman who torment me so unceasingly. But if I am such a faithless cur, then you will not want to know what I saw at the inn—'

'What have you seen?' I asked eagerly, only just remembering to keep staring out across the river.

'Richard and some of the other players were practising the death scene,' Masou told me. 'It is a clever idea – the death looks so real. I do not know who the murderer is, yet I believe I have worked out how the effect was achieved – for if I have a big head, it follows that therein lies a large brain!'

'Ha, ha!' I groaned. 'A funny jest. But do tell me how it was done.'

'The players used—' Masou began. 'But no, I must not give it away, even to you.'

Lady Jane and Lady Sarah walked past close behind us on the arms of their escorts.

'Nonsense, Masou!' I hissed in an undertone. 'You know I will tell no one apart from Ellie.'

'The players and I share the same profession – even if they are not as skilled as me,' said Masou. 'By Allah, I would be letting myself down if I gave away their secrets!' I could hear a laughing tone in his voice. I knew what he was up to. This was no loyalty to the actors. Masou was going to save his information so that he could tease me with it!

'You are right,' I replied with a nod. 'And I would rather work it out for myself anyway. Look, the boats are ready.' And then I swept off to join the other Maids before Masou could get in the last word.

Her Majesty was helped onto the Royal Barge and we hurried to take our places beside her. Mr Secretary Cecil and Lord Robert joined us, the harbingers sounded their trumpets and we were underway.

All playhouses are banned on the north side of the river, in the City of London itself. The Lord Mayor and his aldermen have deemed the theatre ungodly. Her Majesty could overrule them, but she is very wise and does not go out of her way to upset people.

We had hardly left Privy Bridge when there was a great outburst of shouting. We looked back at the bank to see several young men of the Court whipping up their horses. They had quite a ride ahead of them if they were to get to the Key Inn in time for the play. Even if they found room to gallop through the busy streets, which I doubted, then it would take them an age to thread their way through the crowds on London Bridge.

'I warrant they are racing,' chuckled the Queen.

'I will put a silver shilling on Harry Beauchamp to win. He has a fine mare.' Lord Robert and Secretary Cecil immediately dived into their purses to provide their sovereign with the required coin, for of course the Queen never carries money.

'And I say that it shall be Sir Mark Armitage,' declared Lord Robert, taking up the bet. Everyone else joined in the betting, but we all knew that Her Majesty would be the winner no matter which horse came first.

Lady Sarah gazed with dewy eyes at the young men until they were out of sight. 'I do hope Mr Swinburne is the winner,' she sighed. 'He looks so fine on horseback!' Mr Swinburne is Sarah's latest – very rich – admirer.

'Indeed!' muttered Lady Jane, just loud enough for Sarah to hear. 'He certainly looks better the further away he is, and his lack of height matters not when he is on a horse!'

This sudden trip to Southwark has certainly set everyone in a flurry – and not only the Court. It was so funny to see the harbingers being hastily rowed across ahead of us, shouting at the boatmen to clear the path for the Royal Barge and trying to look dignified at the same time. The surprise on some of the boatmen's faces made me laugh. They normally have much more warning of the Queen's intention to take to the barge, and so the river is usually empty. Today, however, the harbingers were having more trouble than Moses did when he parted the Red Sea.

I craned my neck to see the other barges following us. Masou was travelling with my uncle, Dr Cavendish. I was glad that Masou's new position meant that he could come with us.

We made for the landing stage at the Paris Garden Stairs. The harbingers scampered up in a very undignified manner to sound their trumpets for the Queen's arrival. The church bells were ringing away merrily and crowds had formed on the bank to see their beloved Sovereign. I could see men with brooms and shovels still working hard to hide the rubbish before Her Majesty set foot on the south bank. Even so, there was a powerful smell and several people held pomanders to their noses. I wished I had thought to bring one. Secretary Cecil looked most disapproving but he said nothing.

We progressed up the jetty and walked between two crooked houses towards a road that ran parallel to the river. Even though it was quite a narrow alley, it was lined with people cheering. Sometimes Her Majesty stops and talks to her subjects but today she was eager to get to the play. We turned to the left and there was the inn. I was surprised to see that it was rather rundown. I could just make out a key in the flaking paint of the battered sign.

'Hold onto your purse, Grace,' whispered Mary Shelton. 'Even with the Gentlemen of the Guard we may not be safe from pickpockets.'

Mr Hatton, the Captain of the Guard, stood by the gate of the inn. His Gentlemen were holding back the crowds.

Just then there was a sudden sound of hoof beats on the dusty road and the riders from Whitehall arrived at the finish of their race. Sir Mark Armitage was first to ride up.

'Your Majesty, you were right!' lied Lord Robert gallantly. 'Did you not say that he would win?'

The Queen beamed. 'The pot is mine!' she declared, and swept in through the gate.

The players had formed a welcoming circle, and as the Queen walked in, they bowed low. Their faces looked very strange in their heavy make-up. One of them raised his head and, still half stooped, began a welcoming speech for Her Gracious Majesty. I recognized him at once. He was Mr Tom Alleyn, the leader of the troupe, whom we had met at the Palace of Nonsuch. His welcome was long and flowery, and as it was not directed at me, I took the opportunity to have a good look round.

The Key Inn has a large rectangular courtyard

with another gate at the end which leads to the riverbank. This gate was firmly locked with a huge iron padlock to protect Her Majesty, but even so a Gentleman Guard stood by it.

A wooden stage had been built on one side of the yard. There was a cloth at the back painted to look like a forest. Mr Somers often uses backcloths like this when his troupe put on masques for the Court. The courtyard in front of the stage was empty and I could see no sign of seating for the Queen. Was she going to have to stand? Then I saw that there was an open gallery running round the upper floor. A chair with carved arms had been placed in the gallery directly opposite the stage. A red velvet cloth roof was being rigged up over it by a Court servant. It was a Cloth of Estate, embroidered with lions.

Mr Alleyn finished his speech with a flourish. Then the innkeeper shuffled forward to be presented and motioned to the servants, who immediately poured out of the tavern room with wine and mead for Her Majesty and her Court.

Lady Jane shook Mary Shelton's arm. 'Can you see Richard Fitzgrey anywhere?' she asked under her breath.

'He is over there,' said Mary calmly, 'wearing a white doublet. See, he is holding a jewelled casket.'

As if he had heard her, Richard Fitzgrey stepped up to the Queen, bowed deeply and held out the little chest. Her Majesty seemed to sparkle at the sight of him. Richard looked as I remembered him, his black hair worn long around the ears and his bright blue eyes alive with interest.

'O Gracious Queen,' he declaimed, 'Your Majesty would do us the greatest of honours by accepting this chest as a memento of your visit. It is a faithful copy of the one used in *Intrigue*.'

I believe Mr Alleyn must have been hoping for an invitation to the Court from the Queen and thus had the casket copied in readiness. I do not think he could have knocked it together in an hour! The Queen thanked him. She is always most pleased with the many gifts she is given, and she always makes the givers feel happy and important. She moved on to speak to the players and I saw that Richard Fitzgrey was having speech with Mrs Champernowne. She soon flapped over to us, looking rather pink.

'The Queen is taking her place in the gallery,' she squawked. 'Make haste, girls!'

We climbed the narrow stairway to the gallery, where doors led off to bedchambers. We took our places on one of the benches that had been placed alongside the Queen's chair. Other members of the

Court filled the other galleries but many had to stand in the courtyard with the ordinary people. There was standing room behind us but it was mainly taken up by the Gentlemen of the Guard.

The Queen looked about her as if missing something. 'Where is my new fool?' she demanded. 'I would have him near me so he can make merry puns for my delight.' And then she looked straight at me. Her Majesty is kindness itself. She knew that Masou would enjoy a good view of the play and so she had ensured it.

Masou bounded up to the bench behind me. 'Your Majesty,' he said with mock sorrow, 'I know nothing of being in an audience. Pray tell me at what stage I must laugh, at what stage I must cry, or applaud, or sigh.' He bowed to the Queen and sat down on his bench – facing backwards and staring expectantly at a chamber door!

Everyone around him laughed, the Queen loudest of all.

'There is but one stage you need, Masou,' she declared, 'and you are always in the centre of it.'

We all laughed and Masou bowed to acknowledge Her Majesty's wit. How clever he is. He had let the Queen top his jest and receive the loudest laughter.

I could not wait for the play to begin. I love all

spectacles and never tire of watching Mr Somers's troupe, but this was different. A *murder* play! I thought it would be fun to puzzle out a pretend mystery instead of a real one for a change. It was a pity we were seated on benches because I could not help fidgeting with excitement.

'Sit still, Grace!' hissed Lady Sarah, glaring at me. 'You will have us all over!'

I almost laughed out loud at the thought of Lady Sarah, me and the other Maids on our backs with our feet waving in the air! What would Her Majesty say?

Nothing was happening on the stage, so I decided to sit on my hands and watch the fun going on in the courtyard below. Sellers were pushing their way among the crowds, stopping with their trays next to those who looked to have plenty of money! They were selling sugared ribbon sweets, pasties and sweetmeats.

The Queen sat forward eagerly, waiting for the play to start, despite Secretary Cecil tutting in her ear.

'My Liege, forgive me for my insistence on this matter,' he was saying, 'but if Your Majesty were to agree to leave on the instant, we would soon be far from this pestilential place.' He held a handkerchief up to cover his nose. 'These common playgoers' –

he waved disapprovingly at the crowd below —
'display all manner of disease and wanton
behaviour.'

I held my breath. The Queen hates being told
what to do. But instead of exploding, she merely
smiled and patted Mr Cecil's hand. 'Be calm, dear
friend,' she said. 'Most of your common playgoers
are members of my Court!'

My belly chose this moment to start growling
and everyone looked at me.

'It is so long since dinner that I am hungry
again,' I explained.

'As always!' commented Lady Sarah, raising her
eyebrows.

'Well, I am still growing and need my food,' I
retorted.

Masou stepped to the front of the gallery and
leaned over the balustrade to attract the attention
of a stout old woman swathed in a cloak. She was
carrying a tray of fruit to sell, but she appeared as
deaf as a post for she took no notice of Masou's
shouts. Eventually he leaped nimbly up onto the
balustrade and shinned down the wooden struts to
the courtyard. He had barely left when his head
appeared again in front of us and he held out a
hand full of beautiful apricots. He presented one to
the Queen, but when we all reached for the rest,

he pretended to slip. Then he got up onto the balustrade and juggled them, to the Maids' delight. Lady Jane shrieked when he pretended to let an apricot fall into her lap, and everyone clapped as he finished and handed one to each of us. I ate mine rather too quickly and got juice down my gown.

'You are most fortunate to have these apricots, ladies,' said Masou. 'The seller was so stiff and slow of movement that I thought she would seize up before I could buy her wares. And the sight of her hairy face under her hood almost sent me fleeing!'

Our laughter was interrupted by a loud drumroll. Masou scurried to his seat; the play was starting. I felt a thrill of excitement as Mr Alleyn swept onto the stage and bowed low. He stood beaming and bowing for some minutes. Then someone coughed from behind the stage and he remembered that he had a play to introduce.

'Your Majesty, my lords, ladies and gentlemen of the Court,' he began, 'I have a tale that will amaze you. A tale wherein lies a mystery to be solved. You are about to witness a foul murder!' Lady Sarah gasped at this, I know not why. She knew full well what the play was about. 'Any who can guess the identity of the murderer shall win a prize.' The audience clapped and Mr Alleyn bowed a few more times, then flung out an arm. 'Let me transport you to the mythical kingdom of Silverland, where lived Count William, the richest man in all the realm . . .'

Richard Fitzgrey strode out onto the stage. I must admit he looked magnificent with his white doublet and the sparkling rings on his fingers. Under his arm he carried a jewel-encrusted casket just like the one he had presented to Her Majesty. He was certainly enjoying the effect he was having on the ladies, who fluttered and sighed and fanned themselves frantically.

'But Count William had enemies!' declared Mr Alleyn.

Three robed and cloaked figures slunk onto the stage, followed by their servants. One wore red, one green and one blue. Their faces had been whitened and their eyebrows and lips painted on with kohl in sharp lines. They cast threatening looks at Count William.

'These three villains are plotting to kill the Count and steal his treasure,' Mr Alleyn explained, stepping forward.

'Watch closely as our fearful tale unfolds.
The Count will die, but who will deal the blow?
Which of these three men will do the deed?
A purse of silver for the one who knows!'
A loud thunderclap made us all jump, and rain

started to fall! Some of the audience held out their hands and looked up at the sky. I realized that the 'rain' was only falling at the back of the stage. But it looked so real, it was amazing!

'How is this contrived?' I gasped.

'It is simple, ladies,' said Masou, making sure he was addressing us all and not me alone. 'There are towers on either side of the stage, hidden to us by curtains. Between the two is laid a wooden trough with holes. When water is run through it, the rain falls like magic! And the sound of the thunder is made by a metal sheet.'

So much for keeping the secrets of the troupe! I thought to myself.

As the storm raged, the three cloaked villains huddled together and plotted. Each swore to the others that he would share the treasure if he was the one to kill William. But, to the audience, each whispered that he would keep the booty for himself. Behind the three stood their servants, rubbing their hands greedily.

There was a bang and a cloud of smoke and we all jumped. When the smoke cleared, there stood the blue enemy glowering at the audience. He crept up on Count William and swung a log at his head. But Count William had chosen that moment to bend down and pick a flower. The log missed, of course, and hit the blue enemy's own servant instead – much to the amusement of the audience.

No sooner had Count William given the flower to his wife than the green enemy crept up and hid in a large barrel, clutching a sword. The audience had already seen that the green villain was adept in swordsmanship, so we knew that Count William was in grave danger. However, Count William's men arrived and took the barrel away to be filled with beer. The green enemy waved frantically from the top of the barrel as it was carried off. The audience laughed loudly, and the troupe kept breaking into rousing songs, accompanied by musicians who played from one of the galleries.

Then the villains became more earnest in their endeavours and the audience's laughter slowly died. The red enemy tried to lure Count William into a river where he would drown. The water was portrayed by shimmering blue silk moved by unseen hands. It looked fast and dangerous. But the red enemy fell in instead and made a great show of drowning. His servant dived in to rescue him, but he disappeared as well.

The villain in green (who had obviously escaped from the barrel but was now dripping with beer) tried to run Count William through with a sword, but accidentally tripped and – to the audience's delight — ran himself through instead. We all cheered at his demise, and Mrs Champernowne exclaimed — a little louder than she meant — that he deserved it!

The green enemy's servant dragged the body away. If I had been William, I would have been quite pleased at my enemy's death, but not him! He gave a kind-hearted speech, saying, 'I do most heartily grieve for this man's wife and little ones. I will not see them starve.' As he spoke, I noticed that Richard Fitzgrey was playing to the Queen alone. And Her Majesty loved it.

We were then entertained by a long song about sunset and sunrise, and a wooden sun moved across the stage a few times.

Suddenly a shout went up and the red enemy's cloaked body was dragged on stage to lie at Count William's feet.

William made a noble and sorrowful speech. 'How fate doth shape our lives! This second knave would have killed and robbed me, yet within a few days the river hath done the same to him. It drowned and bloated him, and robbed him of his looks, so none can say for sure "I knew that man".'

Now only the blue enemy remained. He made a big show of taking two identical goblets and putting poison into one of them. Then he asked the Count to drink a toast with him. William took up the goblet with the poison but a messenger came in and he put it down again. Then the servant came over to take the goblets away and the blue enemy had to stop him. By now the goblets were thoroughly mixed up and the audience gasped as Count William took one and drank deeply. He began to cough and the blue villain smugly snatched up the other goblet and drained it. Then William stopped coughing – he had merely drunk too fast – and a look of horror came over the blue enemy's face. He clutched his throat and died.

When the clapping had stopped, William stepped to the front of the stage and spoke. 'Gentle folk, it grieves me that three should wish me ill when I have done no harm to them. Why do they strive for my demise? Could it be for this box of treasure? Sad mortals, to crave wealth above honour!'

There was a cheer from the audience and the musicians struck up another rousing tune. The players gave voice to a merry song about how William had beaten all his enemies.

I knew this could not be the end. We had been promised a murder. William made a speech about how he loved the wonderful realm of Silverland

and how lucky he was in his glorious monarch. He went on at length about all the Queen of Silverland's attributes, looking up at Her Majesty all the while to show who he was really talking about. Her Majesty nodded and beamed, which I think encouraged him to elaborate his speech even more.

'. . . and I would lay my treasure at her feet, for she is the glorious sun!' he cried, flinging his arms up towards the painted sun on the backcloth. 'The blessed sun that shineth upon—'

Thud! An arrow suddenly struck Count William in the chest. He cried out as if in terrible pain and fell to the floor, where he lay perfectly motionless as red blood seeped all over his white doublet. Although the audience knew that Richard was acting, his death was so realistic that we gasped in surprise. I decided I would pester Masou until he told me how the illusion was achieved.

Mr Alleyn stepped onto the stage. 'Poor Count William is gone,' he declaimed in mournful tones. 'Killed by a deadly arrow – but whose hand pulled the bow?'

I was determined not to be beaten by this puzzle. I have solved real mysteries and I was sure this one could not be so very difficult. We had been shown three villains and one of these had killed Count William. An idea was nagging at the back of my mind, but I had no chance to think about it, for suddenly a man dashed onto the stage carrying a bow and arrow. He must have been the one given the task of firing the deadly missile. I was about to applaud him, for he had shot very true, when I saw that he had a look of horror on his face. At first I thought that this was part of the play, but the actors on stage seemed puzzled by his arrival and Mr Alleyn tried to wave him away.

The man did not go. He fell to his knees beside Richard, grabbed his doublet and shook him. Richard was limp in his grasp. The man jumped back, white with shock. He looked around wildly and suddenly seemed to realize that the eyes of the whole audience were upon him. He let out a horrified yelp, dropped the bow and arrow and fled from the stage.

The audience muttered in confusion, but I kept my eyes on the motionless body on the stage. I could see that the red liquid was spreading slowly and thickly over the boards. The crowd near the stage were pointing at it, enjoying the horror of the moment, but a cold feeling crept over me. How could this be a trick?

Mr Alleyn walked over to William, bent to look at him and then recoiled in terror. His voice was shaking as he called for silence. 'We are witness to a terrible tragedy,' he told us brokenly. 'And it is not part of our play. Richard Fitzgrey is dead!'

A few moments later

Fran just came in and I was so engrossed in reliving the horror of that moment that I jumped and made a line across the page. She has finally gone – after uttering a thousand apologies for startling me, even though I told her it mattered not.

As soon as Mr Alleyn had made his shocking announcement there was uproar. Richard Fitzgrey, beloved by all, had been killed in front of us! Worried servants poured out of the drinking room, and ladies were screaming. Ladies Jane and Sarah sobbed hysterically, and there were no young men nearby to comfort them so I realized they were not pretending! The Gentlemen of the Guard immediately drew their swords and moved to protect the Queen. They made a wall around her and the rest of us had to move out of their way and bunch up by the stairs. The players stood helplessly on the stage, not knowing what to do.

I could not believe such a terrible thing had

happened. And in front of the Queen! I knew that a crime committed so close to Her Majesty would be investigated most seriously by the Board of Green Cloth. I could hear Mr Hatton's voice above the din, giving orders to his men at the gates.

'Close and seal the inn! Let no one leave this place. Morling, Fairbrother and Kineton, set to and find the man who fired the arrow.' He looked up towards the gallery.

Mr Secretary Cecil called over the heads of the guards, 'Your Majesty, I would counsel you to leave this accursed place on the instant and return to the safety of Whitehall.'

I did not hear the Queen's reply, but the next moment we were all flattening ourselves against the inn walls to allow her to pass. I saw the expression on her face, and I could tell that Her Majesty had no intention of scurrying back to Whitehall, whatever Secretary Cecil might say. Her Gentlemen of the Guard were rushing along to catch up. Mrs Champernowne gathered Lady Jane and Lady Sarah close to her, clucking nervously at the rest of the Maids to come and follow the Queen.

The crowds fell to their knees as Her Majesty swept through to speak to Mr Hatton. He was trying to get some sense out of Mr Alleyn, who was immediately prostrate at the Queen's feet.

'My Liege . . . how can this have happened in your royal presence?' he gabbled. 'I do not understand why Cyril Groome – that is the man who fired the arrow – I do not understand why he should have killed Richard . . . But he must have meant to kill him, for I can see from the arrow shaft that it is not the false and harmless one that we use for the play—'

'Enough, man!' snapped the Queen. 'Calm yourself and allow Mr Hatton to go about his business. The culprit will be apprehended in no time, will he not, my good Captain of the Guard?'

'Most assuredly, My Liege,' said Mr Hatton. 'With your permission I will start by examining the body.'

The Queen nodded and he vaulted onto the stage. He bent over poor Richard and looked hard at the arrow and the wound. 'He has been struck in the heart, Your Majesty,' he reported. Then he struggled with the knots of a purse on Richard's belt, freed it and looked inside. 'Here is our motive, I fancy,' he announced, holding it up. 'Cyril Groome murdered Mr Fitzgrey for his money. That's probably why he ran onto the stage after firing the fatal shot. This is a tidy sum of silver. Men have been murdered for less. But he was foiled. The purse was tied on too firmly for him to grab it and make off with it.'

'Heavens be praised that the crime is solved so simply!' declared Carmina, fanning herself with relief. 'Clever Mr Hatton. All that remains is for the culprit to be caught – which will not take long, I fancy. Then we can sleep easy in our beds.'

I did not make any answer. Others may have been satisfied with the explanation given but I was not so sure. Cyril Groome was a member of the troupe and had surely worked alongside Richard every day. He must have had ample opportunity to do the deed in private and escape without being seen. Why shoot a man on stage and run on to steal his purse in front of the audience, including Her Majesty? It did not make sense. But one thing was certain. The Queen's peace had been troubled and she would need my services as her Lady Pursuivant.

Mr Hatton came back to the Queen and they had a murmured conversation. Mrs Champernowne had her hands full with my Ladies Jane and Sarah, who were still hysterical. This was my chance. I caught Masou's eye and nodded towards the stage. We slipped through the throng and climbed the wooden steps to where Richard lay, staring sightlessly up at the sky. I felt very sad looking at his crumpled body.

'My poor friend,' Masou said brokenly. 'Why would Cyril want to do this to you? I can only think he picked up a real arrow by mistake. But no – he would have seen the sharp point.'

'Masou, you must tell me now how the death scene was meant to be achieved,' I said firmly. I was determined to seek justice for Richard Fitzgrey.

Masou reached out a hand and gently touched Richard's doublet. 'He has thick leather padding here, over his belly. It is hidden by his costume. Between the doublet and the padding is concealed a bladder full of pig's blood. When I saw the rehearsal, the false arrow struck him here, bursting the bladder and making it seem that he was bleeding. Richard told me that Cyril had fired it at him a thousand times and the trick had never gone wrong.'

Masou mimed how the arrow would hit the padding.

'Wait,' I said. I stared down at the arrow and then over at the side of the stage where Cyril was meant to have stood. Masou had mimed the arrow hitting the padding as if it had come from there. But I realized that if Cyril *had* shot the fatal arrow from the side of the stage, then the arrow in Richard's doublet would now be pointing directly at the sky. But it was not!

Masou looked at me. 'What is it, Grace?'

'Cyril could not have shot the arrow from the side of the stage,' I whispered to him. Masou looked puzzled. 'Imagine I am Richard making his last speech.' I stood as Richard had stood and mimed an imaginary arrow plunging into my chest, to lie at just the same angle as the real one. 'The arrow hits me like this, and must have come from' – I followed the angle with my finger – 'that top corner of the stage, behind the curtain!'

'That curtain hides one of the towers I told you of,' said Masou, 'where the players stand to pour the water into the pipes and make the rain.' He looked down at the arrow in Richard. 'I believe you are right, Grace. The arrow *was* shot from above!'

'And if it was Cyril, why would he bother to go up the tower to shoot Richard when he had ample opportunity to do it from his usual place?' I reasoned. 'Moreover, why did he then run onto the stage for us all to see – with another arrow in his hand, besides?'

'I heard Mr Hatton suggest that the miscreant had that second arrow just in case he needed another shot,' said Masou.

'I cannot believe that,' I replied. 'My instinct

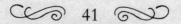

tells me this is not as clear cut as it looks.'

'I do believe you are right,' agreed Masou. 'For the arrow Cyril was holding was the prop for the performance. It could not have done poor Richard any harm.'

This was certainly a matter for the Queen's Lady Pursuivant. I left the stage, went straight to Her Majesty and curtsied deeply. The Queen did not look in a fair mood. She had Mr Secretary Cecil at one ear and Lord Robert Dudley at the other, and they were both urging her to leave forthwith.

She saw me and silenced her two faithful councillors. 'Save your breath, gentlemen. Your advice is falling on deaf ears.' She looked sharply at me. 'I hope *you* are not also going to tell me what to do, Lady Grace,' she said.

'No, indeed, Your Majesty,' I replied in a low tone. 'But I would speak to you about this murder. I have some misgivings . . .'

'You saw the murder as well as I, Grace,' the Queen murmured so that I alone could hear. 'The villain showed himself to the whole audience. Be assured Mr Hatton will shortly bring him before me. You need not trouble yourself with this matter.'

I curtsied as she turned back to her companions, but I was not going to let the matter rest. I reasoned that the Queen had not actually *forbidden* me to carry out an investigation. Indeed, I would be failing in my duty as her Lady Pursuivant if I did not search out the real wrongdoer. I wanted to hear Cyril's story for myself. There was too much at odds here for me to believe him guilty. I found myself watching the other actors. Was one of these the murderer?

Mr Hatton was just approaching the Queen when a Gentleman of the Guard, Edward Fairbrother, came rushing up, red in the face and out of breath.

'We can find neither hide nor hair of Cyril Groome, sir,' he puffed.

'God's oath!' railed Mr Hatton. 'This is intolerable. I will not have him escape!'

'Your Majesty should leave at once,' insisted Lord Robert, 'for we cannot be sure that the arrow was meant for the actor and not a more illustrious victim.'

The Captain of the Guard looked shocked. 'Are you suggesting, my lord, that this was an attempt on the life of our Gracious Sovereign? If so, 'tis better that every actor here be thrown in the Tower!'

'Mr Hatton!' The Queen's tone was cold. 'I will not have you fill the Tower with these players. It is clear that the arrow was not meant for my person, but for that of poor Mr Fitzgrey, and I would not wish a false report of an assassination attempt to be whispered throughout Europe. I would not give my enemies false hope – or, indeed, ideas!'

Secretary Cecil nodded gravely. 'That is wise, My Liege,' he said.

Lord Robert grunted. The Queen took his arm. 'We will away to Whitehall, Robin, for I am weary of Southwark. Mr Hatton, close up this inn until this unfortunate business is concluded. And if you wish to detain the players, bring them to the palace. There is room enough to put them in the Banqueting House and you can question them at your leisure.'

I felt sorry for the players. The canvas Banqueting House is all very well when we go in there for our dessert after a feast in the cool of the evening, but on a hot August day it would be a furnace! However, it occurred to me that it would now be an easy matter for me to speak to the players and find out more about Cyril Groome and any others who might wish Richard harm.

The Queen moved towards the gate we had entered by. I wished I did not have to leave with the royal party. I would have liked to take a good look round for clues that might show the truth about the murder. As I reluctantly joined the other

Maids, who were already following Her Majesty, I heard the concerned mutterings of the inn staff and players alike.

'How will I make a living if my inn is closed?' moaned the innkeeper wretchedly.

'At least you will still have your freedom,' said the actor who had played the red enemy. 'Who knows what awaits us at the palace?'

Mr Hatton and his men began rounding up the players. As I left the inn courtyard, I heard him shout, 'Bring every weapon used in the play. In fact, everything belonging to the troupe is to be brought along, down to the last false beard!'

I am relieved to have finished writing of Richard Fitzgrey's sorry demise. There has been no news of Cyril's arrest, but no matter, I will speak to the actors who are now kicking their heels in the Banqueting House. I need to find out exactly where Cyril was when the arrow was shot. And I have a perfect excuse to venture outside. When I was making my way up to my chamber to write this entry, Mrs Champernowne asked me to walk the Queen's dogs, but said I was to wait until it became cooler. I think the time is just right now – and I will take Ellie with me, for I may need her help, and four ears are better than two.

Heavens! What a poor friend I am to her. She will have heard the news of Richard's death by now and I know she was very fond of him. My dear Ellie could be grieving as I write. I must go to her.

Just before supper
In a window seat outside my bedchamber

We are about to go to supper and I am the only Maid ready. I wish Mrs Champernowne would come along now and see that!

Walking the dogs this afternoon has left me with even more questions! Before fetching little Henri, Philip and Ivan, I went in search of Ellie. She was sure to know about Richard Fitzgrey's death by now. I found her in the Still Room, furiously pounding lavender. The moment she saw me, her eyes brimmed with tears. I put my arms around her and let her cry her fill.

After a while she sniffed loudly and rummaged in her apron. To my surprise, she produced a handkerchief – she generally used the back of her hand – and proceeded to blow her nose loudly.

''E was an 'andsome man, and no mistake,' she

hiccupped. 'And now 'e's been done to death!'

'I am so sorry I was not the one to tell you,' I said.

'That's all right, Grace,' she sniffed. 'There's no stopping news, especially bad, from flying round this place. We all knew something was amiss when all the players suddenly arrived. For a moment I thought we was going to see the play, but then someone said that Richard . . . was . . .' She gulped hard. 'I 'ope that Cyril gets what's coming to 'im. 'E deserves it all and worse.'

'Hush, Ellie,' I said, stroking her hand. 'Never fear. We are going to find the murderer.' And I told her how I believed Mr Hatton was after the wrong man. 'How would Richard lie easy in his grave with an innocent man hanged and the murderer still at large?'

'I'll help you,' Ellie promised.

'In that case, off to the Banqueting House to talk to the players – if they have not suffocated already from the heat!'

'It's not so bad,' Ellie insisted. 'They could have all been thrown in the Clink! The Banqueting House is like a palace in comparison. But how can you talk to the players?'

'I have been instructed to walk the Queen's dogs,' I said. 'If they should take us by the

47

Banqueting House, then we are only doing our duty.'

We collected Philip, Henri and Ivan. The dogs were pleased to be out, as always, but I felt sorry for them with their thick fur. I took them first to the fountain in the Privy Garden so they could drink to their heart's content.

I was relieved to see that the players had been given the liberty of the courtyard outside the Banqueting House. They stood in clusters, arguing loudly, although their words were not so much angry as fearful. From what I could hear, they were complaining that all their belongings were in a storeroom under guard, and they dreaded being hanged because of Cyril. Some of Mr Hatton's guards were watching them. I held the dogs' leashes tightly and pulled them towards the nearest group. The dogs did not seem to mind — there were bushes in the courtyard, and it was as good a place as any to leave a doggy scent.

The actor who had played the red enemy was holding forth to a group of friends. He was still in his costume and his make-up was running with sweat. He looked most bizarre. He declared for all to hear that Richard must have been murdered for his purse of silver. 'I did not know Richard to be wealthy but, trust me, money will have been Cyril's motive. It always is in cases of murder.'

I too had been wondering about Richard's full purse. Actors were not known to be wealthy.

'You've been playing too many bad characters, Ned,' said another actor, who wore a breastplate. I thought I remembered him being at the back of the stage – playing a soldier maybe. 'Cyril wouldn't hurt a fly. He must have picked up the wrong arrow, that's all.'

'Mayhap he'd had too much ale,' said another. 'I just can't see Cyril wanting to do that to poor Richard. It must have been an accident.'

Henri had finished with the bush and suddenly seemed to notice all the strange new people. He wagged his tail excitedly and pulled me towards another group.

'Careful, my lady.' Samuel Twyer, one of the Gentlemen of the Guard, stepped forward. 'I advise you not to get too close to these players. Cyril Groome may not have been working alone.'

But I needed to get nearer so, in case Samuel should think of stopping us, I surreptitiously let go of Henri's leash and he bounded forward.

'I have little say in the matter, Mr Twyer,' I answered, with what I hoped was a foolish giggle. 'Lord Henri here is as determined as his Royal Mistress. I can only follow where he leads. And I am sure he would bite hard if anyone tried to harm me.'

'Then I will not stand in his way,' laughed Samuel Twyer.

Clever Henri! I will save him some choice cuts of meat from our meal tonight. For, as if he had read my mind, he led us to a player who was ghoulishly regaling his fellows with his thoughts on the murder. I bent and pretended to fiddle with Philip's collar, pulling at Ellie's sleeve to bring her down with me. Philip immediately rolled on his back and Ivan and Henri followed suit, so, while pretending to be engrossed in scratching their bellies, we were able to listen to the players.

The young man seemed very excitable. 'Was I not standing right next to Richard when he was so foully slain?' he was declaring to the man who had played the green enemy. 'That arrow could have been meant for me! I saw the blood spurt from poor Richard's chest, and heard the rattle of death in his throat!' He flung out his arms in dramatic fashion at these fanciful words.

Of course, I did not believe that he was the target but I remembered he had indeed been on the stage at the time. He might have seen something that would help my enquiry. I quickly looked round to make sure that Samuel Twyer was out of earshot, then stood up and stepped into the group, with Ellie close behind.

'Please forgive me for interrupting,' I said, 'but your words greatly interest me – the murder has the Maids all in a flutter. Tell me, what is your name?'

The young man was obviously flattered to find that one of the Queen's Maids of Honour wanted speech with him. 'John,' he said, quickly snatching his hat from his head. 'John Winstone.'

'Well, John,' I said, 'we all saw the murder from the gallery, but surely you must have seen more . . .'

John Winstone puffed out his chest and did a little swaggering walk around his companions. 'Did I not tell you I were going to rise in the Company?' he told the others. 'Now I have noble *ladies* wishing to hear my thoughts on this matter.' He suddenly remembered his manners and swept me several huge bows.

'Do you know who shot the arrow?' I asked him.

'Of course it must have been Cyril,' declared John.

'But did you see the moment when he let loose the arrow?' I persisted.

'No,' John admitted. 'I was too busy playing "Friend of Count William of Silverland".' He

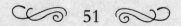

winked at Ellie. 'A very important part, I might add.'

I saw Ellie raise an eyebrow. She was clearly not impressed by this strutting player.

'Then it might not have been Cyril who shot the arrow?' I suggested.

'It had to be, my lady,' said John, scratching his head. 'I saw him in his usual place at the side of the stage just after the fatal shot.'

'Aye, I saw him too,' the green enemy put in, nodding in agreement.

'I remember it as plain as day,' said John dramatically. 'I were stood by the painted tree and Richard were on my right.'

'He was not,' declared Green Enemy. 'He was on your left!'

John looked uncertain and held his hands up in front of his face. He looked from one to the other, frowning in concentration. At last he smacked his palm to his forehead. 'That's the truth,' he acknowledged, grinning at us. 'I'm always muddling my left and right!' He looked as if he were going to launch into a story about other times when he had got muddled, but I wanted to talk about the murder.

I had to know if it was possible for Cyril to have done the deed from the tower and then quickly got back to his usual position before anyone saw him up there. I quickly put in another question. 'Could Cyril have fired the shot from somewhere else?' I asked, looking fascinated. 'From the tower, for example? And then quickly climbed down to be seen by you at the side of the stage?'

John laughed and shook his head. 'No one can get down quickly from that tower. I know it well. You see, my lady, it is one of my tasks to be up there pouring water into the pipe to signify rain in the storm scene, and then I have to get down again to beat the drum for the dancing. Well, going up and down the ladder inside the tower is not something to do in a hurry if you value your health. It's dark and you have to watch where you put your feet and there's a wicked old nail poking out. When I was making my way down after doing the rain tonight, I got a nasty gash from it and bled like a—' He suddenly remembered he was speaking to a lady and rambled on instead about how he was by Richard's side at the very moment of the murder.

I pretended to listen, but I was actually thinking that it didn't seem possible that Cyril had shot Richard, then climbed down from the tower and been standing at the side of the stage in time for

John to see him. And this could only mean one thing: Cyril had not fired the fatal shot!

I motioned to Ellie. We drew away slightly, and I told her of my doubts. 'Yet one thing puzzles me,' I said. 'Why did Cyril flee if he did not kill Richard?'

'Because he thought Mr Hatton would blame him no matter what,' Ellie suggested. 'After all, he was holding a bow and arrow!'

John Winstone was still talking to his friends and I didn't want to miss any clues, but I also wanted to listen to Red Enemy's group – they were still talking loudly about arrows and blood.

'Ellie,' I whispered, 'we need to be in two places at once! Take Ivan and loiter near that first group of players for me.'

Ellie nodded and set off, Ivan trotting by her side. Green Enemy bent down to greet Philip and Henri. The two dogs must have recognized someone who would give them a hearty scratching, for they rolled over again.

'Good boys,' said Green Enemy. 'Stout fellows!' Without ceasing his petting, he looked up at John. 'What were you doing on stage anyway?' he asked. 'I thought you'd be playing your pipe for the final song.'

John grinned. 'Mr Rouse paid me to take his

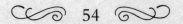

place on stage in that scene,' he explained. 'No one knew it were me for I wore his armour and helmet and didn't have any words to say. I were glad to do it. I'm not going to spend my life throwing rain and drumming and tootling on the pipe. I want to be an actor.'

If I had been one of the dogs, my ears would have pricked up at this. Who was this Mr Rouse and why had he wanted John to take his place for the final fatal scene? Was it because he had to be somewhere else at that time? Up in the tower, firing a fatal arrow at Richard, perchance?

'Well, the play was no worse for your taking part,' laughed Green Enemy. 'Bartholomew Rouse is a terrible actor!'

'I reckon I played it much better,' John Winstone declared in agreement. 'I'm going to ask Mr Alleyn to let me do it from now on.'

'Excuse me, John,' I said quickly, wanting to find out more. 'Which player is Bartholomew? I was just wondering . . .' John and Green Enemy were looking at me intently – of course, I could not tell them I was investigating the murder. I thought quickly and came up with: 'You see, I did feel there was a change in the performance of the "friend" that you were playing, and indeed it was much better in the final scene. From what you say I will want to avoid Mr Rouse's future performances at all costs!'

John was delighted with this. 'I'm going to tell Mr Alleyn that an' all!' He beamed, then looked around the courtyard. 'That's strange. I don't see Mr Rouse here.'

'Nor I,' said Green Enemy. 'Indeed, I haven't seen him since poor Richard died.'

I had to stop myself from exclaiming out loud. This was very suspicious. It was quite possible that Mr Rouse had paid John to take his place in the play, then climbed up the tower and shot Richard. Then he could have made his escape before anyone had realized that Richard was truly dead. The main gate had not been sealed until after the murder was discovered, and the Gentlemen of the Guard would have been stopping people only from coming in, not from going out. My theory would certainly explain why Bartholomew Rouse was not rounded up and brought to Whitehall with the rest of the players.

Ellie returned to my side then and begged a word. It took a few moments for us to move away from the players, as Philip and Henri were reluctant to leave their newfound friend, and then Ivan wanted to meet him as well. At last we contrived to drag them away.

'I have heard a name,' Ellie whispered. 'Bartholomew Rouse.'

'I too,' I told her. 'And no one has seen him since before Richard died. It is suspicious. We must find him.'

Ellie grinned broadly. 'I know where he lives!' she hissed delightedly. 'One of the players said he's been renting a room in the Bull boarding house, right close to St Paul's Cathedral.'

At this moment Henri gave a growl and we turned to see Mr Hatton approaching. This was good fortune. I could tell him all I knew and he could send his men to find Mr Rouse and question him. But Her Majesty's Captain of the Guard did not look pleased to see me. I believe he was finding this whole business very frustrating.

'What is this twittering Maid doing here, Twyer, and why are we awash with puppies?' He glared at me. 'I suggest you take the Queen's dogs away from these ruffians, Lady Grace, and go . . . sing some madrigals or something!'

Faith! I could not stay after being so dismissed. If only Mr Hatton knew what I had discovered, he would not have been so quick to send me on my way.

As it was, Ellie and I made our way back into the palace without another word to him. It was time to return the dogs and make ready for supper.

Back in my chamber, Ellie took an age over my hair but I decided my white gown looked well enough for the evening meal so I did not have to change.

Ellie and I had a little tussle over this. I believe she thinks more about my appearance than I do!

'What will Her Majesty think of me?' she exclaimed as she tried to untie my sleeves. I could tell she was not pleased. 'She'll be throwing me back in the laundry, you mark my words, if I send you to table with the dust of Southwark on you.'

'Then you may brush my gown and change my wrist ruffs,' I told her, 'and if the Queen says anything, I will tell her how you tried to improve me.'

'And if she says anything to *me*, I'll say you are the most difficult lady I've ever 'ad to dress!' Ellie declared. She put her hands on her hips. 'Well, I'm sure you would be if I'd dressed any others!'

I burst out laughing and Ellie had to see the funny side. She brushed me down and changed the ruffs and I was at last able to come here to this window seat and escape the hubbub. Ellie is now helping Olwen with Lady Sarah, who has decided to change her dress as she 'cannot be seen in one at a play and the same at supper'. Olwen tried to persuade her that different sleeves would do as there was not much time, but no, my finicky lady must have everything changed, from partlet to petticoat. At least this time it will not be me who keeps everyone waiting.

Hell's teeth! Lady Sarah has just poked her fine head out of the door of our chamber. 'Scribbling away again, Grace?' she said. 'You are always keeping us waiting!'

If I was not so fond of this daybooke, I believe I would have thrown it at her head! But I must put it away and get to supper.

Late, past eleven by the chapel clock

I am in my bed and have one small candle so that I do not disturb Lady Sarah and Mary Shelton, who are asleep.

All through supper I wondered about Bartholomew Rouse and how I could find out more about him. After the meal I went in search of Ellie. I wanted to contrive a way of getting inside Mr Rouse's lodgings and searching for evidence. If only I could leave the palace at will, like Mr Hatton, but as a Maid of Honour I do not have that freedom and must use all my wits to slip away unnoticed. It is likely that Mr Rouse is now in hiding, but if he is in his lodgings, I will not hesitate to face him. He will not be the first murderer I have dealt with! I looked in my bedchamber for Ellie, but there was no sign of her. Then I met Olwen in the passage outside.

'Have you seen Ellie?' I asked.

'She said she was going to the pantry, my lady,' said Olwen, bobbing a quick curtsy.

'The pantry?' I echoed.

'Yes, my lady. She said she was going to practise. I know not what she meant. Is there something I can help you with?'

'No, thank you,' I said quickly. 'It is not important.' And I hurried away.

I passed the Great Kitchen, where the servants were at table, and poked my head round the door of the pantry. To my surprise Masou was sitting there on a stool with a large brown wig on his head! And behind him stood Ellie. She was carefully entwining a ribbon into the horsehair. It was an extraordinary sight and I burst out laughing.

'I was told you were practising something, Ellie,'

I chuckled. 'I never expected you to be turning Masou into a Maid of Honour!'

Masou stuck his tongue out.

'Masou is being very helpful, Grace,' she rebuked me, reaching for a looking glass to show him her handiwork. 'I can practise hair fashions all I want and *he* knows how to sit still, unlike some!' she added darkly.

'But I have sat still for long enough!' said Masou, grinning. 'I must stretch or walk like an old man for the rest of the day.'

Ellie sighed but carefully took the wig off his head and put it away in a basket. Masou jumped to his feet and went through some strenuous exercises.

I perched on the stool for a minute. Ellie's eyes lit up and she reached for her comb.

'There is no time for that,' I said, and added quickly, 'Much as I would *love* another new hairstyle. But I am glad to find you both together. We must seek out Richard Fitzgrey's real murderer.'

'Ellie has told me everything you found out, Grace,' panted Masou as he stood on his hands. He sprang to his feet again. 'So unless Cyril practises the dark arts he could not have been in two places at once.'

'What do you know of Bartholomew Rouse?' I asked.

'I have heard the name,' said Masou, 'but that is all.'

'It matters not,' I sighed. 'Ellie and I will just have to go to his boarding house as soon as we can. I will think about how that can be contrived. It will be difficult.'

'And foolish,' muttered Ellie. 'You're talking about going to see a murderer!'

'What else can we do?' I shrugged. 'Come, Ellie, help me make plans.'

We had just reached the staircase by the Great Hall when we met Mrs Champernowne. She looked flustered.

'There you are, Grace,' she said. 'Listen hard. We are attending a service tomorrow morning at St Paul's Cathedral. Her Majesty has just decided. We leave at ten and I must tell all the Maids.' She started up the stairs and turned. 'Ellie, you will make sure your mistress is ready in time, look you. Now where are Lady Jane and Carmina?'

She bustled away, talking to herself under her breath. Poor Mrs Champernowne. She finds it hard when the Queen gives her short notice of anything – and that is often!

I think I know why the Queen has a fancy to

visit St Paul's. The cathedral spire was destroyed by lightning when she was a child. Her Majesty gave a large sum of money towards the rebuilding costs, but still there is no spire. I think her visit is more to check up on her investment than for the sermons – hence her decision to attend with so little warning, which gives the Bishop no time to dream up excuses. But of course that suspicion of mine must remain within the pages of my daybooke!

Whatever the reason, it is good news indeed for me, as it has made my task much easier. 'We have no need of plans now, Ellie,' I said joyfully. 'They are made for us by Her Majesty. I will attend the service and then surely I can find a way to absent myself from the royal party and visit Mr Rouse's boarding house.'

'You make sure you take Mary Shelton with you,' ordered Ellie. 'If I can't be there, you must have someone else sensible.'

I will make sure I am awake early and ready to go to St Paul's in the morning. I find I cannot wait to go to church – which is most unlike me!

The Twelfth Day of August, in the Year of Our Lord 1570

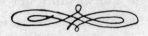

In the Great Hall. Dinner time

It is near to one in the afternoon and I am at table. So much has happened that I must write it down while I can. I could have sat in the quiet of my bedchamber, but that would have meant missing my dinner.

Ellie woke me early this morning so that she had plenty of time to attend to my hair. I wore my white dress again and sleeves with pale green net over. The net had come from a dress of my mother's. Ellie had a whole basket of trinkets that she wanted to thread into my hair. I was determined to sit still but it was not easy, especially when one of the clips caught in the back. There must have been quite a tangle, for she combed and combed! Thankfully, Mrs Champernowne had made sure that some breakfast was sent up to us or I would have fainted with hunger.

It was almost ten when Ellie handed me my glass. Beneath my hat, my hair was loose and looked prettier than usual. Ellie's lime-wash mixture had made it shine and the little silver trinkets were charming.

I believe Lady Sarah was quite envious of me. Olwen is a very good tiring woman but she does what she is told while Ellie has ideas of her own. That is perfect for me, for I have not a clue what looks well and what does not. So I think it was jealousy that prompted Sarah's words when she patted the back of my head.

'Charming, Grace,' she simpered. 'And I am sure tangly bumps will soon be all the fashion!'

Without thinking, I put my hands up to feel. There was a lump of hair where the clip had caught.

'It is lovely, Ellie,' I said loudly. 'Just what I wanted.'

Of course I did not want a strange lump in my hair, but Ellie had tried very hard.

Mrs Champernowne bustled in and hurried us down to the palace gate, where our horses and grooms were waiting.

Soon we were on our way to the City. Harbingers sounded the procession. Her Majesty, dressed in a magnificent silk cloak embroidered all over with lions rampant, rode with Lord Robert and Mr Hatton by her side. The Gentleman Guard were around her and we Maids came behind. We made slow progress, which pleased me as I do not relish being on horseback even with old Tom, my groom. Her Majesty insists that her Maids ride pillion for processions like this. She is a very fine – and daring – horsewoman but she does not trust us to stay in the saddle!

The route was lined with people cheering the Queen. As we passed the Charing Cross, one little girl was lifted up to present Her Majesty with a limp bunch of pink gillyflowers. The Queen took the bouquet as if it were made of rubies and thanked the child, who beamed at her.

We rode on again through Temple Bar and into Fleet Street. It was very hot, and although I did not wish to sit through a long sermon, I looked forward to the coolness of the cathedral.

At last we came through the gate at Paul's Chain and I looked up at the old Norman church with its spire-less tower. We dismounted and Mrs Champernowne hurried us inside. There was the usual bustle in the church, with fashionable stalls set up in the side chapels and traders calling their wares. The Queen took her customary seat close to the pulpit. We went up to the covered gallery in the north transept. There were times when we could not hear a word of Bishop Sandys's sermon for the noise of the congregation and the shoppers below. I am not the most patient person at the best of times, and today I was particularly eager for the sermon to be over so that I could search for Bartholomew Rouse. Each time the Bishop paused for breath, I thought he had finished and was ready to jump to my feet for the final prayers. But then he began to speak again.

Mrs Champernowne looked at me crossly several times, then reached across Mary Shelton and pinched my arm. 'Sit still, Grace!' she hissed.

At last the service came to an end. It was clear that the Queen wished to speak with the Bishop.

'Do you think Her Majesty is going to demand answers about the spire – or lack of it?' whispered Carmina.

'She has a very determined look on her face,' Mary Shelton replied.

'I am glad I am not in his shoes,' I put in. I hoped the Queen would give him a lengthy lecture, for I had a boarding house to seek out!

Mrs Champernowne hurried us to the side chapels. 'We will await the Queen's pleasure here,' she said, looking eagerly around the stalls. 'Do not go too far, ladies.' And with that she bustled off towards a glover.

Lady Jane and Lady Sarah followed her, with

Carmina in their wake. Now was my chance to slip away to the Bull boarding house in search of Mr Rouse. I asked one of the stallholders if he knew where I might find it.

''Tisn't far, my lady,' he told me, beaming. 'Just through the west door and down Ave Maria Lane.'

I thanked him for his information and quickly moved away before he should wonder why a Maid of Honour would wish to venture down a dingy alley. I looked for Mary Shelton, as Ellie had advised. I found her at a stationer's booth looking at some sheets of vellum and pulled her away by the sleeve.

'I need you to help me,' I whispered. 'I have to go somewhere and I cannot go alone.' I linked arms with her and led her past the other courtiers and out of the west door.

'Where are we headed?' murmured Mary Shelton, blinking in the bright sunshine.

'I cannot explain everything. I'm sorry,' I added ruefully, for Mary is so patient with me and I wished I could tell her more. 'But I have to go to the Bull boarding house, just down this street.'

Mary smiled and patted my hand. 'I will ask no more,' she said. 'Only that you do not hurry me. It is far too hot to rush!'

Many delicious moments later

I had to stop, for a servant just approached our table and I had to choose between blackcurrant tart and trifle. This was a hard decision. After careful consideration I plumped for the tart. Before writing again, I had to lick the red-stained clotted cream off my fingers, and that set Mrs Champernowne glaring! Of course, I then used my napkin and finger bowl, but at least I had not wasted any of the wonderful taste.

We found The Bull easily and I knocked upon the door. After a while it was opened by a large woman in a brown hemp dress and a dirty apron.

'Who goes there?' she growled in a very unfriendly voice. Then she squinted at us in the sunlight. I could see her taking in our fine clothes and her tone changed. 'My ladies' – she bobbed a quick curtsy – 'what can I do for you?'

'I am looking for Bartholomew Rouse,' I said.

'You and me both!' the landlady laughed sourly. 'I 'aven't seen 'im since yesterday and the rent's due

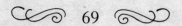

on 'is room. I'd let someone else 'ave it, but it's full of 'is belongings. 'Tisn't right. I'll be throwing it all out if 'e's not back tomorrow.'

So Mr Rouse had disappeared. I did not need much more convincing that he had murdered Richard Fitzgrey, but I did wonder why. Had Mr Hatton been right? Had Mr Rouse killed Richard for his purse of coins, or was there some other dark business between the two men?

'That is bad indeed,' I murmured sympathetically, and Mary Shelton nodded in agreement. I thought quickly. I wanted to get past this woman and search Mr Rouse's room. 'I have business with Bartholomew,' I said. 'He borrowed my . . . brother's hat . . . for his play-acting and my brother must have it back. If I could just make sure it is not in his room . . . ?'

I admit that seeing my excuse written down shows it for the lame thing it was, and certainly Mary Shelton raised her eyebrows at me, for she knows I am an only child, but luckily the landlady did not notice, especially after I had pressed some pennies into her hand.

The woman showed us up a rickety staircase to a small room at the very top of the house. I think she wanted to stay and see what we were up to, but Mary came to my rescue.

'Have you some small beer or mead?' she asked. 'My throat is parched.'

The landlady led her off down the stairs, eager to make more money.

Mr Rouse's room was very hot and stuffy. There was an unmade bed, two large chests, which seemed to be full of clothing, and a battered old table. I knew the nosy landlady might return at any minute once she had given Mary her mead so I had to be quick. The table was strewn with papers. I did not like to look through another's personal things – after all, I would hate anyone to pry into this daybooke – but there had been a murder and I wanted to find the villain, so needs must. I quickly leafed through the papers. There were letters, playbills and accounts – nothing that seemed important to my investigation.

Then a name jumped out at me from the desk: Richard Fitzgrey. There it was in ink, his signature at the bottom of a letter! This was important. It proved there was a link between him and Bartholomew Rouse. I picked up the letter to read it, but at that moment I heard a tread on the stairs. I hurriedly slipped it into my sleeve just as the landlady opened the door. I expressed sorrow that I had not found the hat and pressed a few more coins into her eager hand.

'*Did* you find your brother's hat?' asked Mary Shelton as we hurried back up Ave Maria Lane. 'I would be astonished if you had, for you would have had to find a brother first!' Then she squeezed my hand. 'Do not worry. I know you will not be able to give me any explanation for our little expedition.'

'It is very important,' I told her. 'That is all I can say.'

'Then that is all I need to know.' Mary smiled and pointed over at the churchyard. 'Look, Her Majesty is only just stepping out of St Paul's. Poor Bishop Sandys looks quite careworn. I imagine he has been harangued this last half-hour.'

We were about to leave the little lane when two men approached. They were roughly dressed and very dirty.

'Spare us a copper, my ladies,' said one, holding out his hand, which was ingrained with grime.

'I'm sure they will,' said the other. He grinned horribly, showing stumps of rotten teeth, then reached inside his tatty jerkin and pulled out a vicious-looking club. He raised it in the air in a threatening manner. 'They won't want to feel my old friend here.'

'Thieves!' whispered Mary. She pressed close to my side.

I was very frightened. These men wanted our purses and seemed determined to get them by any means necessary! Then, stupidly, I began to worry that, in a scuffle, the letter might fall from my sleeve and be discovered or lost. I decided to be bold.

'This is not to be borne!' I declared. I fixed my gaze over the thieves' heads as if I could see someone approaching. 'Why, Sir Pelham!' I called, snatching a gentleman's name from thin air. 'Please come and run your sword through these miscreants for me!'

The villains could not stop themselves from turning to look. In that moment I grabbed Mary's arm and we bolted for the cathedral. The two robbers knew better than to follow where the Gentlemen of the Guard were. When I dared to glance back, they had gone.

'Mary,' I gasped, 'I am so sorry. I led you into danger.'

Mary Shelton had turned pale, but she managed a shaky giggle. 'Oh, Grace,' she said. 'To use Sir Pelham Poucher as your hero!'

As it chanced, we could now see Sir Pelham inside the cathedral. He was at a stall buying sweetmeats. He is old and very stout and not heroic at all.

'Maybe he could have sat on them!' I suggested, and we both went off into peals of laughter – partly for my joke, but largely, I think, because we were both so relieved to have escaped the thieves.

We sank down onto a pew to recover ourselves, and I hugged Mary in thanks. I knew she would not say a word of this to Mrs Champernowne. Indeed, if the Mistress of the Maids were to hear of it, we would never be allowed to leave the palace again. Even though I find her fussing a little over-zealous, she is right about one thing: London can be a dangerous place!

'I must hurry back to the stationer's stall to buy my vellum,' said Mary Shelton a few moments later when the colour had returned to her cheeks, 'before Her Majesty gives the command for us to depart.'

I nodded, and as she hurried away, I carefully pulled the letter from my sleeve. I felt strange reading the words of a dead man but I knew I had to. As I read the first words, I was shocked. The tone of the brief letter was venomous, the sentences short and sharp.

Bartholomew, our friendship is at an end, I read. *Keep your nose out of my affairs, or, by God, I will make you suffer!*

I tucked the letter back into my sleeve. I was

very surprised by it. I remembered Richard as a charming, jolly man, yet when writing this letter, he had clearly been full of anger. In several places he had pressed so hard with the quill that it had made a hole. What had Bartholomew Rouse done to cause Richard to write such a letter?

Just then, Mrs Champernowne called for me to stop daydreaming; the horses were ready to take us back to Whitehall.

Wait! A messenger has just come into the Great Hall and is making his way towards the Queen. I will listen.

Three of the afternoon by the clock

This is my first chance to pick up my daybooke again since the arrival of the messenger at dinner. Her Majesty has ordered that we have a peaceful hour after dinner. We are all in her Presence Chamber, instructed to do something quiet and improving. She said it was too hot for anything else – she was tired of our 'silly gossiping' at dinner. Well, I was not guilty of that, for I was too busy thinking of my investigation most of the time, although Her Majesty might not have been pleased had she known about that!

The Queen is following her own orders very well. She is translating the homily 'Against Idleness' from English into Latin. She is so clever! I know not what the others are doing, but I am improving myself by writing in French. At least, that is what I shall tell anyone who asks! I have an idea: I will mutter some French word now and again as I write, and everyone will think me as clever as our Monarch! *Mon Dieu!* The Queen would not like that either. No one must seem as clever as her. I had better resume my tale before I write something treasonous by accident!

Now, where was I? Ah, yes – I mean, *mais oui* – I was at the dinner table. The messenger entered the room and bowed to the Queen and then to Mr Hatton, who was seated next to her. I did not have to strain my ears to hear him for he had a loud voice and spoke as if he were addressing an army.

'Your Majesty, with your permission I shall deliver myself of an important message to Mr Hatton. Sir, the miscreant Cyril Groome has been found. He is at this very moment in the Clink prison in Southwark. He was apprehended for drunken behaviour and not thought fit to be brought to Whitehall, where he might offend our Gracious Monarch. He awaits you there, sir.'

The Captain of the Guard immediately rose from the table, bowed deeply to the Queen and followed the messenger from the room.

Poor Cyril, I thought, accused of a murder I am certain he did not commit. It was important to clear his name as soon as possible. I knew I must get Mr Hatton onto the trail of Bartholomew Rouse, but of course I could not tell him directly; he would not listen to a mere madrigal-singing Maid of Honour! However, I thought I could *guide* him in the right direction. I decided that first I would make him doubt Cyril's guilt. Then, when Mr Hatton sought a new suspect, I would ensure he happened upon Richard's letter to Bartholomew Rouse . . .

After Mr Hatton had left, there was a hubbub around the room. Mr Swinburne and William Penshawe, who were sitting with us, began shaking their heads and telling us how dreadful life was in prison. I am sure that their stories were for the benefit of certain ladies. Their descriptions became more gruesome with every gasp from Lady Jane and Lady Sarah!

'Fie, William!' exclaimed Mr Swinburne at last. 'Let us talk no more of the piles of rotting bodies

 77

strewn across the floor for the rats to feed upon. You will upset our fair companions.'

'Indeed. Then I will not tell that the rats feed on the living as well as on the dead!' added William Penshawe.

Lady Sarah shrieked at this. Mr Swinburne was very quick to take her hand and pat it soothingly – and for some reason she took a long time to calm down. Lady Jane fanned herself violently, but did not get the same treatment from Mr Penshawe – which was a pity for her as he has a large fortune and she had been trying to catch his eye throughout the meal. Finally she sat with her hands in her lap, looking sour as curdled milk.

I began to feel very anxious for Cyril Groome. I knew that many of the terrible stories I was hearing were true and that there was no pity for prisoners. Even if found innocent, they would suffer if they had not the money to pay for their shackles to be taken off.

Sir Mark leaned forward with an eager grin. 'There was one murderer who was chained to the walls of his cell and forgotten. When the jailers finally remembered him, he was a rotting corpse.' Mr Swinburne was now moved to fan Lady Sarah with his napkin.

'No one had noticed the smell in the general

stench,' went on Sir Mark. 'There were marks on the wall where his starving fingers had scrabbled desperately for life!'

My Uncle Cavendish was sitting across from me. He looked up from his plate and humphed at this. 'He deserved no better. He took a life, and his was taken in return. It was a fair punishment.'

'But suppose he had been innocent, Uncle?' I questioned him.

'That is a different matter altogether,' said Dr Cavendish. 'You know me to be a fair man, Grace. I would not see unjust suffering if it were in my power to stop it.'

My uncle is sometimes heavy with drink, but today his eyes were not bleary and his speech was clear. He is a just man, clever too, and I found myself thinking that perchance he could help me clear Cyril's name. It would not be the first time he has unwittingly helped me to solve a mystery. I felt sure that if I brought the facts before him, he was sober enough to see that Cyril could not possibly have shot Richard. Then all I had to do was make sure he told Mr Hatton. Dr Cavendish has a good deal of influence in Court, and I was sure that the Captain of the Guard would listen to his opinion. But I had to tread carefully; my uncle must not know that I was guiding him to his conclusion.

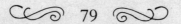

'I hope that Cyril Groome will meet such a fate,' I said firmly. 'Then this sorry business will be over. It grieves me to think of Richard Fitzgrey, lying there on the stage, struck by the fatal arrow. Though I cannot help but wonder how it happened, for did not Mr Fitzgrey wear padding?'

'Mr Hatton said it was a most determined shot,' replied William Penshawe.

'I heard that the arrow did not touch the padding,' Sir Mark put in.

'It pierced the neck and went downwards, straight to the heart,' said Mr Swinburne with relish. He was clearly exaggerating wildly. 'Did you not see all the blood?' Then he remembered his dining companion. 'Pray forgive me, Lady Sarah.'

Mr Swinburne may have been elaborating somewhat, but he had hit on the crucial fact that I needed my uncle to consider. '*Downwards* to his heart, you say . . . ? The arrow struck *downwards* . . . ?' I repeated loudly, in a slow voice.

'Zounds!' my uncle exclaimed thoughtfully. 'There is something amiss in all this.'

'How so, Uncle?' I asked innocently, holding my breath for his next words.

'Consider, child, if the arrow sped across from the side of the stage, it could not have struck Mr

Fitzgrey at much of a *downward* angle. Indeed, it would have been almost perfectly horizontal.' He demonstrated by holding his knife to his doublet as if it were the arrow. Its handle pointed directly across the table at me, and it was horizontal. My uncle was on the right track.

'*That* is not how the arrow was,' insisted Mr Swinburne, pointing at the knife my uncle was holding. 'The arrow pointed downwards into the body, just as I described.'

'He's right. I saw it too.' Mr Penshawe nodded. He had completely forgotten poor Lady Jane. 'It was jutting upwards from the player's chest.'

'So what can this mean?' I asked, as if puzzled.

'Well,' mused Dr Cavendish, 'if the arrow was at such an angle, then it can mean only one thing: the arrow was fired from above.'

'But I do not understand!' I exclaimed, wide-eyed. 'For Cyril Groome was seen at the side of the stage when the murder occurred, not *above* Mr Fitzgrey.'

'These things are not for you to dwell on, Grace,' said my uncle. 'But if what you say is true, then I tell you this – Cyril Groome could not have killed Richard Fitzgrey!'

There was a gasp from those around us.

'Of course, Uncle, I see the truth now that you

have explained it all so expertly!' I breathed. 'How clever of you to work it out!'

'Why, yes, if Dr Cavendish had not been here, we would never have known what really happened!' added Carmina excitedly.

'So Cyril is innocent of the crime!' declared Sir Mark.

This caused quite a stir about the table and I was secretly delighted. But then my uncle settled back in his chair and poured himself a generous glass of wine. He seemed to have forgotten his words about seeing an innocent man suffer.

'You made the explanation seem so clear, Uncle,' I exclaimed. 'Not one of us had thought of it before. And if Cyril Groome is innocent, then the true culprit must be still at large! Her Majesty will be most grateful when you tell her what you have deduced.'

I could see that my words had worked, for my uncle put down his glass and rose.

'I intend to tell her forthwith, Grace,' he said. 'As for you, my dear, think no more about this unpleasant matter.'

I could not agree, of course, so I smiled at him and he seemed satisfied. I watched him bowing to the Queen and bending to speak to her. In an instant she called a page, who listened to her words, then ran from the room in haste.

Heavens! (But I forget my pledge to work in French. I mean *ciel*!) That was hard work! But I have achieved the first part of my goal, for word now buzzes around Court: Cyril Groome is innocent; the real murderer is still on the loose!

The Thirteenth Day of August, in the Year of Our Lord 1570

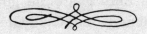

Half after eleven

I have come to the kitchen gardens this morning
to write in my daybooke. It is cool here and I am
shielded from view by a large gooseberry bush.
And as all the fruit has been long picked, it is not
likely that anyone will come this way. Mrs
Champernowne believes me to be with Ellie,
trying on a new linen cap. But I must not tarry as I
have been away so long already!

Last night there was good news but I had no
chance to write of it. The Queen herself
sent a message to Mr Hatton at the Clink
that Cyril Groome was to be released
immediately.

Mr Hatton returned to Court soon after and I
was itching to give him Richard's letter to
Bartholomew Rouse there and then. But I could
not, for I would have had to explain how I came
by it. By the Rood, it is sometimes vexing to be a
Maid of Honour! If I was Captain of the Guard, I

would solve mysteries so quickly that I would not need so many daybookes!

Instead I had to hatch a plan so that Mr Hatton would find the letter for himself, and I could not think how to contrive this. Once or twice I found the Queen's eye on me. It was a thoughtful look. I wondered if she remembered my doubts at the time of the murder and suspected that I might have had a hand in Cyril's release. But she said nothing – mayhap I imagined it.

The Saxon Ambassador is at Court, discussing trade or something like that, and Mrs Champernowne has found out that he has a love of madrigals. She keeps gathering the Maids into a bunch to sing to him. I think it is the Maids rather than the madrigals that he likes – and Lady Jane in particular – but whichever it was, he kept asking for more.

I could not stop thinking about the mystery. It was most embarrassing when I started off '*Weep, weep, mine eyes do weep*' with the wrong chorus at the wrong time and in the wrong key! Indeed, this earned me a hard nudge in the ribs from Lady Jane. Apparently the Saxon Ambassador is a relative of the Elector of Saxony himself and therefore good husband material!

In the end I was grateful to the Ambassador, for

the answer came to me in a song! We had just sung a line about some silly girl's heart being 'locked in a room where none may venture', and it came to me! There was one locked room that Mr Hatton was certain to venture into – the storeroom where the players' belongings are being kept. If I could plant the letter in the storeroom, I was sure that Mr Hatton would find it and be off on Mr Rouse's trail. I was so excited by this that I started singing an extra verse on my own – until I realized that everyone was staring at me.

I whispered my plan to Ellie this morning in my bedchamber. She stopped pinning up the front of my hair and frowned at me.

'You're mazed, Grace,' she told me. 'The room's well guarded.'

I had forgotten that, but I was determined not to be beaten. 'There must be a window,' I insisted.

Ellie thought for a moment. 'I believe there is, but it's small and high up.'

'Then we will need Masou!'

'If he can't get in, no one can,' Ellie agreed. 'I'll go and find him once you're dressed and ready.'

She was just hooking the aiglets of my bodice when Mrs Champernowne came in.

'You are doing well, Ellie Bunting,' she said. 'But, look you, have Lady Grace ready on time.'

'Yes, Mrs Champernowne,' Ellie said, bobbing a curtsy.

I could see she was pleased. She'd never drawn compliments from Mrs Fadget when she worked in the laundry, although she worked very hard. Mrs Champernowne watched as Ellie helped me into my petticoats.

'Your new cap will be ready later, my lady,' Ellie said suddenly. 'I have just got to finish the embroidery, but I am not sure of the size. I may need you to come in a while and try it on.'

I held up my looking glass to try and catch her eye. What was she talking about? I had a pretty net cap all ready to be placed on my hair when it was all pinned up. She winked at me, and finally I understood. Ellie was setting up an excuse for me to meet her and Masou – and with Mrs Champernowne's blessing, it seemed, for the Mistress of the Maids was nodding in agreement.

After breakfast we went to the chapel to listen to a group of St Paul's choristers.

'Bishop Sandys sent them,' whispered Mary Shelton, 'to try and appease Her Majesty for the tardiness of the repairs at the cathedral.'

'They are not likely to lose their place in the music like some Maids!' hissed Lady Jane.

'Nor will they spend all their time preening and

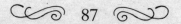 87

trying to catch the eye of the Saxon Ambassador,' added Lady Sarah, smiling sweetly.

Jane threw Sarah a furious look, but before she could say anything, Mrs Champernowne arrived. 'Hush your chattering and pay attention to the music!' she snapped. 'Grace, Ellie Bunting needs you,' she added quietly. 'Go and try on your new coif.'

I had no idea what we were going to do if we had to produce this imaginary coif, but I was not going to worry about that. Ellie led me to the Wood Yard, where Masou was practising his juggling by an apple tree. He greeted us with an elaborate bow.

'Good morrow, ladies,' he called. 'I knew you could not do without the help of the Great Masou and his acrobatic skills for long.'

Ellie jerked a thumb at a window above our heads. 'That's the window to the storeroom where all the players' belongings have been put.'

'Thank you, Ellie,' I said. 'Now I have another mission for you. I need you to wander down to the Banqueting House and ask the players how they are. And if you happen to slip Bartholomew and Richard into your conversation and learn more about either of them, then I will not be sorry. But look you do not bump into Mrs Champernowne, for she will want to know why you are not fitting my new coif.'

'I will be invisible,' declared Ellie, and she set off, slinking against the wall.

I gazed up at the storeroom window. It looked very small and very high. 'Are you sure you can get in there, Masou?' I asked doubtfully.

'There is nothing simpler,' he said, beaming. 'Now where is this letter that is so important to you?'

I gave it to him. 'I need you to place this so that Mr Hatton will find it and then set off in pursuit of Bartholomew Rouse,' I explained.

Masou nodded solemnly, folded the letter and tucked it into his shirt. Then, making sure that there was no one around to see, he climbed up to the window. He found footholds in the brick where there appeared to be none, and made it look very easy. The window seemed to be shut, but this was no problem for Masou. In an instant he had it open – I could not see how he contrived it. It is lucky he is honest, for he would make a quite excellent burglar!

Soon Masou had disappeared from sight. I waited for a moment, but I was eager to see what he was up to, so I hitched up my skirts and pulled myself up into the branches of the apple tree. From there, I could just see into the storeroom if I leaned out rather awkwardly. I must have looked like a performing monkey!

Inside the storeroom were stacked chests, baskets and painted scenery. In the corner was a huge pile of costumes. Masou was bending over a quiver of arrows. I saw him tuck the letter in the top. Well thought, Masou! Mr Hatton would be sure to examine any weapons he found, and therefore would certainly happen upon the letter. I was just about to climb down from the tree when I saw Masou suddenly dart away to the far corner of the room and disappear behind the costumes. What was he up to?

A moment later, the door of the room swung open and Mr Hatton stepped inside. Masou was trapped!

A few moments later

I stopped writing just now because I had the feeling I was being watched, but it was only a tame robin redbreast perched on the gooseberry bush and looking at me with his head cocked. I must be feeling jumpy, writing about poor Masou's plight.

Mr Hatton glanced around the room quickly. He had a grim look on his face and I feared for Masou if he were found. I did not think that Mr Hatton would listen to any excuses. He might even think that Masou was involved in the murder in some way. After all, he had lost his only suspect. Had I led my friend into danger?

The Captain of the Guard moved slowly between the players' belongings. He rummaged through some sacking and looked behind a painted shield. Then he went over to the pile of costumes where Masou was hiding. I held my breath as Masou crept away to duck behind a wooden bush. But now Mr Hatton made his way over to that! Masou had to move again. He dived between a basket and a chest, but as he did so, a goblet on the chest fell with a clatter.

Mr Hatton drew his sword! 'Who goes there?' he cried, spinning round.

He reached forward to shove the basket aside. In my anxiety, I leaned across and nearly fell out of the tree! I thought Masou was going to be run through for sure, but when Mr Hatton moved the basket, there was no sign of my friend. I scanned the room and caught sight of his black hair behind a painted mermaid.

'Damned rats!' exclaimed Mr Hatton as he

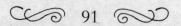

sheathed his sword and moved away. I sagged with relief and realized I had been gripping the branch so hard that my knuckles were white.

Mr Hatton was now standing right in front of the quiver of arrows. I watched as he pulled them out, dislodging the letter, which fell to the ground. I nearly screamed in frustration, for he did not seem to notice it at all.

After he had inspected each arrow head and flight in turn, he looked about as if wondering where to search next. I nearly shouted out, 'Look under your feet!' but luckily I restrained myself, and then he took a step forward, kicking the letter as he did so. That drew his attention at last, and he stooped to pick it up. He began to read and I saw him stiffen as the meaning became clear. Clutching the letter tightly, he turned and strode out of the room. I heard the key turn in the lock, and then Masou popped up from under the skirts of a gown that lay draped over a table. How he had got there I had no idea! He scurried across to the window and was out in a flash. I carefully climbed down from the tree to meet him.

'Did you see my stealth?' he boasted, making bows to an imaginary audience.

'You were wonderful indeed, Masou!' I agreed. 'And now that Mr Hatton has the letter he will

surely set about finding Bartholomew Rouse and the murder will be solved!'

The next minute Ellie was upon us, puffed out with running. 'I have some news,' she panted. 'I have heard that—' She broke off, for we could all hear voices at the far end of the Wood Yard. We fled for the kitchen gardens and the safety of the smokehouse.

'Hold!' I said. 'I am not going in there. I stank like a side of bacon last time.' We squeezed behind the smokehouse instead. 'Now, Ellie, your news.'

'I asked about Bartholomew and Richard,' Ellie burst out. 'They were the best of friends until a few months ago. But then they fell to quarrelling, and all because Bartholomew had fallen in love with Richard's sister, Alice. Apparently Richard was furious, though Alice seemed very partial to Bartholomew and welcomed his suit.'

'So is that why Richard told Bartholomew to keep out of his affairs?' I murmured. 'I wonder why Richard had objections to the match. A fellow player would surely be acceptable as a husband for his sister.'

'Well,' Ellie went on, 'Richard went out of his way to pick arguments – all the players heard them – and he was even trying to get Bartholomew thrown out of the troupe. It surprised people, because everyone likes Bartholomew even if they don't think he's much of an actor.'

'Mayhap there is something sinister about Bartholomew and only Richard knew it,' said Masou thoughtfully.

'Mayhap Bartholomew silenced Richard before he could tell the others,' I added.

'What's our next step?' asked Ellie.

'We leave it to Mr Hatton,' I said. 'Now the letter is in his hands, there is nothing more we can do. He will get the truth out of Bartholomew Rouse.'

I should have returned to the chapel then to hear the choristers, but I wanted to write it all down straight away. The kitchen gardens are peaceful, but there is one thing that troubles me: no one has seen Bartholomew since the murder, so how will Mr Hatton find him?

Mid afternoon

I am sitting in the shade by the Bowling Green and just have time to scribble this. It is important.

We have just returned from a walk in the park

of St James. The Queen said it was too hot to ride, thank Heaven, but she wanted to show the Saxon Ambassador her fine deer. This pleased Lady Jane, and I think he looked more at her than at the deer. Secretly, of course, for he would not want to offend Her Majesty.

As we walked under the trees, my head was still full of the murder mystery. I wondered if Mr Hatton had had time to act upon the information in the letter. I knew I could not ask him outright, but perhaps I could get the information from him in a more round-about way. Then I realized I could not see him in the party. He would normally be close to the Queen. I wanted to know where he was and I knew just who to ask: Mary Shelton.

'It is strange that Mr Hatton is not accompanying Her Majesty,' I said casually, putting my arm through Mary's.

'He is gone in pursuit of a new suspect in the murder,' Mary Shelton told me. 'I am surprised that you did not know, Grace.' She gave me a meaningful look.

'I do not interest myself in such matters,' I said airily. 'But if you wish to tell me, then I will listen politely.'

Mary pinched my arm and we both burst out laughing. She knows as well as I that this is not true. 'A letter from Richard was found,' she went on. 'It was written to' – her voice dropped to a whisper – 'that same Bartholomew Rouse who borrowed your brother's hat! Mr Hatton found out that Mr Rouse should have been standing right next to Richard on stage in the fatal scene, but that someone had been persuaded to take his place. Mr Rouse has not been seen since. Mr Hatton has set off to Rochester in Kent in search of him.'

'Rochester?' I queried, for I had not expected that. 'Why so?'

'Mr Rouse is from that town,' explained Mary, 'and has family living there. Mr Hatton believes he may have slipped away there.'

My thoughts were diverted at this point by Lady Jane, who had got her slipper caught in a tree root and was making such a fuss that the young men of the Court were flocking to her aid. Unfortunately for my fine lady, the Saxon Ambassador did not leave Her Majesty's side, so her shrieks were in vain.

When the Queen had had enough of the heat – for the trees gave us little respite – we made our way back to Whitehall. As we came into the Tilting Yard, a messenger galloped up on a steaming white mare. He dismounted and knelt before the Queen, who nodded for him to speak.

'Your Majesty,' he panted, 'I bring news of Bartholomew Rouse. He has been arrested and is now in the Clink prison.'

'Are you telling me he never left Southwark, man?' demanded the Queen incredulously. 'A bold villain indeed!'

'I do not know his movements, My Liege,' replied the messenger, 'but he was caught riding through the Stone Gate on the bridge. He claimed he was going to his lodgings by old St Paul's.'

'Then Mr Hatton was spared the ride into Kent?' asked the Queen.

'No, Your Majesty,' the messenger told her. 'But we have sent word to him to return.'

My suspect was under lock and key! I was elated, but of course I could not show it. And I did spare a thought for poor Mr Hatton, who had been sent on a fruitless journey on such a hot day.

We continued on our way back to the palace. As we went, Her Majesty beckoned me to her. I had a moment's panic. Was she going to talk to me about the murder? Did she somehow know that I had been investigating, even though she had told me I should not trouble myself with this mystery? But it seemed not.

'How are you finding your new tiring woman, Grace?' she asked.

I could answer this question with no hesitation. 'Ellie Bunting is wonderful, Your Majesty,' I replied. 'She spends hours making sure that my hair is perfect.' I noticed a twinkle in the Queen's eye. 'But it is I who should be praised for the patience I have shown in sitting still while she does it,' I told her.

The Queen threw back her head and roared with laughter.

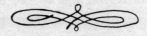

In the Great Hall

It is just after five of the clock and we are sitting in the Great Hall. All the windows are open and there is an evening breeze coming in from the river.

The Maids and the Ladies-in-Waiting are working on their sewing. Her Majesty is embroidering a design of the Wedding at Cana, where Jesus performed a miracle and turned water into wine. She is stitching the water casks at the moment. Mary Shelton has told me that the Queen will give it to St Paul's Cathedral when it is finished. It is a royal hint that if Her Majesty can stitch a picture of the water turning into wine, then they can rebuild the spire. From what Mary says, that would indeed be a miracle!

I have begged permission from the Queen to write in my daybooke instead. I have something very important to record, although I did not tell the Queen that. Her Majesty was in a happy mood after our walk and said yes without hesitation. I wonder how she would feel if she knew that I was writing about the murder. I doubt she would be in such a good temper.

Something very unsettling has happened which revealed that the mystery I thought solved is not solved at all! Less than an hour ago, Ellie and I were walking through the herb garden. We were gathering lavender to put under the pillows of all the Maids.

As we picked, Ellie and I were surprised by the sound of weeping, and at that moment two of the Palace Guard came round the corner, half carrying a young woman. She did not struggle in their grasp but she was in great distress.

'I beg you to let me speak to Mr Hatton,' she sobbed. 'I am Alice Rouse, the wife of Bartholomew.' Tears ran down her face. 'We are only just married, and now you have him locked in the Clink, yet he has done nothing wrong.'

'Be quiet, woman!' growled one of the guards. They dragged her towards the Holbein Gate. Ellie

and I followed, keeping to the shadows. 'Be thankful we are just removing you from the palace and not sending you to join your murderous husband!'

They put her outside the heavy wooden door, locked it and marched off. We heard her pleading cries on the other side.

'She says her name is Alice!' I exclaimed. 'Richard Fitzgrey's sister is called Alice. And you heard that she was in love with Bartholomew Rouse.'

'Got to be the same person then,' declared Ellie. 'They must've got married.'

'Poor woman,' I murmured. 'Only just a bride and her husband sure to die for his crime. We must have speech with her. She may know why Bartholomew was driven to this.'

We scurried to the gate and peered through the bars of the small grille. Alice Rouse was still there, sitting in a sobbing heap a little way down the road.

'Mrs Rouse?' I called softly.

She raised a tear-stained face. I could see that she was a very pretty woman with fine blonde hair, but now she looked dishevelled and distressed. She blinked at us, stupefied.

'Do not fear, Mrs Rouse,' said Ellie gently. 'My

lady only wishes to help you.'

'You are Richard Fitzgrey's sister, are you not?' I asked.

Alice nodded, eyes filling with tears again.

'I knew your brother and am most sorry for his death,' I went on. 'You say you must speak with Mr Hatton, but it seems the guards will not permit it. Mayhap I could pass a message to him.'

Alice took a ragged breath and ran over to us. 'I am living a nightmare!' she wailed, clutching the bars. 'Only this afternoon I was riding across London Bridge with my new husband. We were married two days ago and were full of plans for finding suitable lodgings and' – she gulped hard – 'and . . . suddenly guards appeared, with their swords drawn, and they dragged Bartholomew from his horse. They said he was a murderer and' – she gripped the bars so tightly that her knuckles turned white – 'they said he had killed Richard.' She stared wildly into my eyes. 'So in an instant I am told that my dear brother is dead and that my new husband, whom I love as life itself, is the killer!'

'What double tragedy for you to bear!' I murmured.

'But Bartholomew is innocent, my lady,' sobbed Mrs Rouse. 'I am certain it is so, for Richard was

on stage, alive and well, when we left the inn
together.'

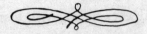

A moment later

Servants have just come in with watered wine. I
downed mine in one gulp.

Alice Rouse was keen to tell us her story. 'We
eloped,' she said. 'Richard would not consent to
our union so we believed it to be the only way. We
planned it carefully. When Richard was safely on
stage for the final scene, we slipped away from the
inn. We knew he would be oblivious to everything
but his role. Bartholomew paid John Winstone to
take his place in that scene and we went directly to
St Saviour's Church near London Bridge, where
we were married.' Her eyes shone with tears. 'The
priest would vouch for us, I am sure.'

'What did you do then?' I asked.

'Bartholomew had hired horses and we rode
straight to Epsom,' sighed Alice. She had a dreamy
look in her eyes. 'My godmother lives there and
she was privy to our secret. I am not much of a
rider, but we made good time and were there for
supper. We made merry with her and her family.

We stayed in Epsom for two nights until we had enough courage to come back and face Richard.'

My thoughts were racing. Alice Rouse sounded most sincere and she would know that it took but a word with the priest of St Saviour's to prove her story false or true. It sounded as though Bartholomew Rouse could not have shot the arrow, for he was being married at that very moment. I felt wretched, for it was my meddling that had caused Bartholomew to be thrown in the Clink.

'I believe that your husband *is* innocent,' I said gently, and I saw relief flood over her face. 'Yet someone did the foul deed. Can you think of anyone who would want to murder Richard?'

'No one!' Alice exclaimed. She sounded sure, but I saw something flicker across her eyes, as if she doubted her own words.

'You can tell us,' urged Ellie. 'You don't want Bartholomew to suffer for something he hasn't done, do you?'

'And think of poor Richard,' I added. 'You want his death avenged, I am certain, and we will need to find your brother's true murderer in order to prove Bartholomew innocent. Forgive me these questions, but did Richard have any enemies?'

'Michael—' Alice began, but then she stopped with a shake of her head.

'Michael?' I said encouragingly.

'I should not say anything,' Alice burst out. 'For I would not cast aspersions on one who may be an innocent man . . .'

'Of course you would not,' I assured her. 'But Mr Hatton must follow up every clue or he may miss the truth.'

Alice took a deep breath. 'Michael Fenton – I was once betrothed to him,' she began. 'He is the third son of Sir George Fenton. He did not get along well with Richard. It was common knowledge. They had even been seen shouting at each other in the street.'

'Why did they quarrel?' I asked. My pulse was racing at this news.

'We were hand-fasted about a year ago,' explained Alice. 'We did not tell anyone outside the family. This was hard on Richard, who was very keen on the match and wanted to tell the world. Sir George is wealthy and I suppose it would have been good for our family – the rise in station, I mean. Then, in April, Mr Fenton broke off our betrothal and Richard was furious. I have never seen him so angry.'

I supposed Richard had been angry for his

sister. Hand-fasting is a serious promise to be wed and should not be broken.

'What did Richard do?' I asked. This sounded most intriguing.

'I do not know. I told him to leave the matter. I had only agreed to the hand-fasting because Richard desired it, and in May I met my dear Bartholomew and we fell in love. After that I had no desire to marry Mr Fenton and was happy to relieve him of his promise. But Richard was still angry! I know not if they saw anything of each other after that.' Alice clasped her hands together around the bars. 'Please, help me free my husband.'

'I will do all I can,' I promised.

'I thank you, my lady,' she murmured. She turned to go and then seemed to remember something. 'How strange . . .' she said. 'In all the confusion I had forgotten. My husband may know more about Mr Fenton and his relationship with Richard, for I saw him talking with Michael a few days ago, and their voices were hot.'

'Do you know what they were talking about?' I asked Alice.

Alice shook her head. 'They broke off when I approached, but I am sure I heard Richard's name mentioned before they saw me. Mr Fenton left without another word and Bartholomew looked grave. I asked him what it had been about and he smiled and said it was no matter for me to worry about, and then he kissed my hand and I forgot all about it — for I was to be married the next day.'

We heard a movement inside the gatehouse.

'Go now!' urged Ellie. 'And have faith. All will be well.'

Alice left and we hurried away from the gate.

So now I sit here berating myself — in writing — for being an addle-pated fool! I proved Cyril innocent by pointing the finger at Bartholomew Rouse, and now I believe that I am wrong and Bartholomew is not the murderer. Another innocent man is in prison, and this time it is my fault!

I have to undo this wrong. And for this I will turn my attention to Mr Fenton. I know that he broke off the betrothal to Richard's sister and angered Richard. But that would give *Richard* a motive to kill, not Mr Fenton. What more is there to uncover? I wonder. I must be sure to move carefully. I cannot afford to make another mistake and cause another innocent man to be accused.

I do not know much of this gentleman, Michael Fenton, but I know exactly who to ask. He is unmarried and of noble birth, so he is sure to have

come to the attention of my fine ladies, Jane and
Sarah!

A little later

I have heard some important information and will
have to act upon it. I am not sure I am looking
forward to that because— But no, I must record
how I came by this information first.

Her Majesty grew tired of stitching her Wedding
at Cana. When Mr Secretary Cecil arrived with
papers for her, she threw down her work and rose
very eagerly. We rose too and curtsied low until she
had left the room. Mrs Champernowne bade us
continue with our work, but as we settled on our
cushions again, I realized that now was a good time
to ask about Mr Fenton.

'Something is puzzling me,' I said airily. 'I keep
hearing the name of Michael Fenton and cannot
for the life of me remember him . . .' I made sure I
spoke his name loudly so that everyone heard it
and could comment if they would.

Lady Ann Courtenay was the first to speak. 'You
must have seen him at Court, Grace,' she said. 'He
is a well-looking young gentleman, the third son of

Sir George Fenton. He lives alone in one of his father's houses. It is on London Bridge. It is the former chapel of St Thomas of Canterbury converted to a house.'

I knew the house and it surprised me that I did not know Mr Fenton, but then I do not gaze at all the young men as some of the other Maids do.

'He has no fortune,' Carmina broke in, 'and he will inherit nothing from his father as he is not the oldest son. Yet he is ambitious. Mayhap that is why he is going to marry into a wealthy family.'

'Indeed, he is engaged to Catherine Lloyd,' put in Lady Sarah. 'Her father is a merchant and often at Court. She is his only living child.'

I nodded. I had seen *her* at Whitehall.

'Word has it that Mr Lloyd is not at all pleased about his daughter's match,' said Lady Jane. 'He is a very strict father and does not think Mr Fenton good enough for her.'

I am grateful that everyone else knows the gossip at Court. It makes gleaning information a lot easier! And they had not finished with Mr Fenton yet.

'I heard it took Catherine a deal of pleading to prove that she truly loves Michael Fenton,' said Mary Shelton. 'She had trouble persuading her father that he is an honourable gentleman.'

'No doubt Michael being the son of a knight was what convinced her father in the end,' laughed Lady Ann.

''Tis a pity he is betrothed, Grace,' said Jane. 'A third son would be a perfect match for you — or at least for him!'

I thought of reminding her that I was goddaughter to Her Majesty, and an heiress to boot, and had no need to throw myself away on a third son (or on any man for that matter), but in the end I ignored her.

'He is a tall gentleman,' put in Lady Sarah, 'with fine legs. You could do worse for looks, Grace.'

I always try not to fall into a discussion about whom I shall or shall not marry. It is of no interest to me. I insist that I would rather stay at Court for ever with Her Majesty, but no one believes me.

Luckily Carmina came to my rescue. 'Mr Fenton may have fine legs,' she snorted, 'but they have been used to pursue most of the ladies of the Court this past year!'

The others nodded at this. No one seemed to have a very high opinion of Mr Fenton.

I had one final question. 'Was he at the play?' I asked. They all looked at each other as they tried to remember. 'I do not recall him being there,' said Mary Shelton finally. 'Besides, Mr Lloyd does not approve of play-acting and I imagine Mr Fenton would wish to please him, so perhaps he did not attend.'

They began to chatter about other such fortune-hunters and I stopped listening and took up my quill.

Everything is such a puzzle. Why should Michael Fenton have wanted to murder Richard Fitzgrey, especially now that he is to marry an heiress? Michael was not seen at the Key Inn, though I suppose he could have been hiding in the tower with his bow and arrow, but why? Perhaps Richard was Michael's rival for the hand of Catherine Lloyd; Richard was certainly ambitious. But no, surely no woman of wealth would consider marrying a humble actor.

And I must not forget that Michael was once hand-fasted to Alice. Where does that fit in? And why were Michael and Bartholomew arguing about Richard on the day before the murder, when Alice said she heard Richard's name mentioned?

I need more information, but I believe that Alice has told me all she knows. There is only one person who may know more, and that is Bartholomew. I shall have to speak to him myself. And in secret, of course!

But the thought of what I must do makes me hesitate. If I am to speak to Bartholomew, I must go to the Clink, and yet the tales I have heard of prison life make me think I should not venture near the place! What terrible sights will I see there?

But I must not think in this way. It is because of me that Bartholomew stands accused of murder, so go I must. Of course, the Queen would be horrified if she found out, and would most likely set me to copying Latin texts for the rest of my life. Worse, I might lose my role as Her Majesty's Lady Pursuivant. No, it is essential that this venture remain top secret. The Queen must never know.

Heavens! I will have to miss supper if I am to get to the Clink before curfew. What a terrible thought. Still, as Lady Pursuivant I must make sacrifices. Ah, me, I can feel a summer fever coming on. It is not so bad that I shall need any nasty physic, but bad enough for me to take to my bed and miss supper. At once.

The Fourteenth Day of August, in the Year of Our Lord 1570

In my bedchamber

It is after noon and I have only just woken. I am mazed with sleep! Ellie has brought me some manchet bread and small beer to make up for my missing supper, breakfast and dinner! So now I have breadcrumbs all over my sheets. Most uncomfortable!

But no matter. I must record every detail of my adventure before they fall out of my head like rotten apples from a tree.

Last night I told Mrs Champernowne that I had a fever and would go to bed directly. She was for calling my Uncle Cavendish but I told her that all I craved was sleep. She reluctantly agreed, but bade Ellie keep a close eye on me.

As Ellie was helping me up the staircase to put me to bed, I quickly told her that my chill was just a ruse and that I planned to go to the Clink. She dropped my arm as if I had the plague.

'I don't need to tell you what will happen to

you if you go there,' she hissed. 'The minute you step through the door you'll be clapped in irons, and you'll have no food and you'll get boils and you'll die. And don't think I'll come visiting!'

'I shall not be locked up,' I protested. 'I shall dress as a servant boy and say I am taking something to my master, Mr Rouse. I have dressed as a boy before and not come to any harm.'

'But not in such a hellhole,' insisted Ellie.

'Dear Ellie,' I said, 'I know you have my interests at heart, but I am resolved to do this.'

'S'pose you'll be wanting me to get the clothes,' grumbled Ellie. 'But I'm not cutting your hair like I did for your capers last year, Grace. If it gets any shorter, it'll be the devil's own job to dress it!'

'Thank you, Ellie,' I said. 'I knew I could count on you.'

'Hold hard, Grace,' Ellie declared. 'I have two demands if I'm to help. Number one, I come with you, and number two, Masou comes with both of us. We'll all be servant boys. Give me a while then meet me in the Buttery,' she added before I could protest. 'You know, by the Wood Yard.' With that she hastened away.

As soon as I reached my chamber, I stuffed my bed with my winter cloak and a blanket to make it look as if I were sound asleep. I placed one of my lace caps just peeking out over the bedclothes. I'm proud to say that it was most realistic and I almost expected the lump to breathe! Then I crept along the endless passages down to the Buttery.

Ellie was already there with a pile of rough, dirty clothes. She wrinkled up her nose at the thought of wearing them and I had to hide my smile. Ellie is very fastidious now – since she has become my tiring woman she notices these things. She helped me out of my gown and farthingale and petticoat and everything, and put them under the bench, covering them with a piece of hessian. I put on rough breeches, shirt and jerkin and Ellie did the same. We rammed caps over our hair and I tucked my purse deep within my jerkin. Ellie produced some battered old boots. They were a little tight but they would have to do.

'Where are we meeting Masou?' I asked.

''E's gone to get us a boat,' said Ellie, pulling my boots on for me. 'For how else do we get across the Thames without going all the way to the bridge? I hope 'e doesn't find one and we have to stay 'ere!'

'Really, Ellie?' I grinned at her. 'No adventure? Would you rather have a humdrum life for ever more?'

'Well, no,' she admitted. 'It's just that I don't

much fancy the idea of going to the Clink. But me and Masou won't let you go there on your own.'

I gave her a hug. 'You two are my best friends,' I told her. 'What would I do without you?'

'Well, you wouldn't get across the river for a start!' Ellie giggled. 'Come, we can't keep Masou waiting.'

She took me down a narrow passage that I had not seen before. But that was no surprise; Whitehall Palace is vast – the size of a village! Soon I was completely lost. At last Ellie pushed open a door that had not been moved for a while. Ivy clung to it on the other side and it scraped open. I couldn't believe my eyes. We were outside the walls of Whitehall!

The river glinted in the evening sun a mere twenty paces away and I could see a landing stage. It was the Whitehall Stairs, downriver from the palace. It was still light and before curfew so the banks were busy. No one took any notice of two urchin boys hurrying along beside the water, though. We had not gone far when Ellie stopped, then spat on her hands and rubbed them in the dirt.

'Got to hide that fine skin of yours, Grace,' she said, smearing muck all over my face and hands, and then on her own. (The thought of the spit was

worse than the dirt, but I did not tell Ellie that!)
'And get some soil under those manicured nails.'

There was a whistle from one of the boats moored at the landing stage. I looked over to see Masou waving cheekily at us. 'Perkin! Norbert! Over here, lads!' he called.

'I'll give 'im Perkin and Norbert!' muttered Ellie out of the side of her mouth.

We raced along the jetty. I was beginning to suspect that there was something alive in my clothes because they itched so much, but I was enjoying the freedom of not having to hitch up miles of petticoat and skirt when I ran. I recognized the waterman – or rather water*boy*. It was Kersey, and we had used his boat before. It was a rough little craft with a sail, though there was no wind today. I was about to greet him when I remembered that it was Lady Grace he had met before, not a smelly little kitchen boy! I pulled the cap further down over my face.

Ellie clambered down into the boat and sat near the bows. But I stopped, waiting to be helped in as I usually was.

'Don't worry!' called Kersey. 'Me boat don't look much but it's watertight, that's for sure.'

There was nothing for it. I had to get in on my own. I could see Masou grinning broadly behind

Kersey as I half jumped, half fell into the bottom of the boat, making it rock violently.

'Fear not, Kersey,' laughed Masou, grabbing my arm and hoisting me roughly onto my seat. 'Norbert is a little simple, but he will do as he is bidden, I hope. Sit still there, Norbert.'

I had no choice but to silently accept Masou's teasing.

Kersey pulled at the oars and we set off.

'As I told you, Kersey,' Masou went on, 'we are on an errand of mercy. Norbert's uncle is in the Clink and we have to take in money for his food. Norbert begged to come, though to tell the truth I would sooner have gone with Perkin alone.' He waved an arm towards Ellie. 'This fine young man works with him in the palace kitchen and keeps him in order there. It is only in the streets that Norbert grows wild and cannot be controlled.'

It was Masou's good fortune that I could not reach his shin with my boot!

The journey was much less stately than in the Royal Barge. The wake of other craft buffeted us and we were quite wet by the time we reached the Barge House Stairs, a little way upstream from Paris Garden. Masou and Ellie stepped out.

'Come, Norbert,' said Masou, holding a hand down to me. I ignored it and made my own way onto the small jetty, slipping onto my hands and knees in the green slime from the high tide. Masou gave Kersey some coins and asked him to wait.

'Thanks, Masou,' said the young boatman cheerfully. 'Be 'appy to wait for that. Good luck with Norbert. It's very charitable of you to take 'im on.'

As soon as we were out of sight of the landing stage I turned on Masou. 'Wild, am I?' I snorted. 'Out of control, am I?'

Ellie and Masou burst out laughing.

'Indeed you are, Master Norbert!' spluttered Ellie. 'With your green-stained breeches and cap all askew, and your hair tumbling over your face. If you could see yourself!'

I quickly poked my hair back up inside my cap. I tried to stay cross, but in the end I had to laugh at their merry faces.

I soon stopped laughing, though, as we made our way onto the road towards Southwark. When I had come to see the play with the Court, we had been safely surrounded by Gentlemen of the Guard, but this time was different. Now it was just the three of us. There were people passing between the taverns and others lurking in the long evening shadows. I knew these could be pickpockets – and worse. I had not forgotten my close encounter with the thieves outside St Paul's! Although my purse was safely hidden under my jerkin, there might be those who would think nothing of attacking a defenceless boy to find out what he was carrying.

Masou sensed that I was uneasy. 'Stay close to me, Grace,' he murmured. 'Keep your head lowered and move along quietly. Then you will go unnoticed.'

Ellie went to slip her arm in mine and then decided that boys would not do that. Instead, she gave me a friendly punch which made my arm throb, but at least I forgot my fear. 'A little care, Perkin!' I hissed. 'Norbert may break loose at any moment. Then what would you do?'

'I'd teach the little urchin how to speak like an urchin!' whispered Ellie. 'So as 'is high-bred tones don't give 'im away.'

'Upon me loif!' I said aloud. 'I 'ad quite fergot!'

'And if you think that is how an urchin speaks, God help us all!' whispered Ellie. 'You'll have us thrown in prison for your terrible mimicking. It's an assault on the earholes.'

We were approaching Paris Garden and it had become even more crowded. A little seed of fear began to grow in my belly as I thought of the prison.

'I have heard it will be dreadful in the Clink,' I said.

'Life in any prison is wretched,' replied Masou, and there was a note of warning in his voice. 'You will not like what you see. But we are only going as servants, not prisoners. There is one thing though: we must beware the curfew. It is at ten of the clock. You must be quick in your enquiries. We will need a hefty bribe if we are to leave after then.'

'Wait!' I said, stopping suddenly on the road. I recognized this place.

'What is it, Grace?' asked Ellie.

'We are at the Key Inn!' I exclaimed. 'Let us see if we can get inside. We were rushed away before, but now we have the opportunity to look for clues. We may find something that helps to clear Bartholomew's name and leads to the identity of the true murderer.'

'Have you forgotten, Grace?' said Masou. 'The inn was stripped of all the players' belongings. Surely there can be nothing left that is of use to us.'

'The Gentlemen of the Guard may have missed something,' I insisted. 'But I will go alone if I must.'

I knew that would do the trick. Ellie and Masou never like to be left out.

The Key Inn was deserted. Every window on the ground floor had been hastily boarded up and the building had a strange gloomy look in the twilight. How were we going to get inside? I wondered.

Masou sauntered up and down. I knew he was searching for a way in but did not want any passers-by to realize that.

'Aha!' he said, diving down a quiet alley. 'Someone was careless. A window is open above.' We followed him down into the gloom. He stopped by some barrels and held his hands like a stirrup so that we could step up onto them. He needed no such help to join us. Then he pointed out that, by using the drainpipe, and then a prominent beam, we could climb up to the window.

The drain was wobbly and the beam full of splinters. The window made a loud creak as I pulled it fully open and climbed inside. I fervently hoped that there was no one to greet me!

At last we were all inside a dark bedchamber with an unmade bed and a close-stool. Judging by the smell of urine, the servants had not had time to empty it when the inn was closed. I held my nose.

'Puts me in mind of the laundry,' whispered Ellie. 'Nothing like old pee for getting rid of stains!' She tried to sound jolly, but I knew she was nervous.

Masou opened the door and we stepped out onto the gallery. Below us lay the courtyard and the wooden stage. The darkening sky gave very little light, and as I looked at the shadows on the stage below, I could imagine shady figures hidden there.

Ellie shivered beside me. 'To think,' she whispered in my ear, 'this is the very place where poor Richard got killed. I 'ope 'is ghost don't walk. I forgot to bring my charms to keep us safe.'

'Hush, Ellie,' I said and took her hand. 'There is nothing to fear here.' I was thankful she could not hear my heart thumping!

Masou pulled out his tinder box and lit a little candle stub. Ellie rummaged in her shirt and pulled out two more. She had also thought to bring some strips of cloth to bind the bottoms of the candles, so that we could hold them without burning our hands on the hot wax.

'You are a genius, Ellie!' I told her.

'What about that, Masou?' Ellie declared, forgetting her fear. 'You always tell us that *you* are the genius. Seems I've taken your place!'

'A true genius such as myself does not boast of his prowess.' Masou grinned.

We all felt better now we each had a light. We found a wooden stairway to take us down to the empty courtyard. The ground was still strewn with the audience's discarded food from the day of the play, and it was beginning to rot in the heat. I went across to the stage, startling the rats who had been feasting on the rubbish and making them swarm away like a moving carpet.

While Ellie and Masou looked around the courtyard, I climbed onto the stage and shone my candle into all the corners. But it was empty. The guards had done a good job of collecting the players' belongings. Then I searched the place where Cyril had been standing. There was a box lying at the bottom of the tower. Perhaps there was something inside! But when the candlelight fell on it, I could see that it was just a fruit seller's tray with a pile of squashy apricots inside. The rats had not found those yet, I thought. I felt sorry for the seller who had been done out of the chance to make some money from them.

The only place left to look was the tower from where the fatal arrow had been shot. I was holding my candle, so I only had one hand free to climb the ladder inside the narrow tower, and it was not easy. I realized that a grown man would have found it a very tight squeeze. At the top was a small platform and I could see that the place was well hidden from the audience and would give a good view of the stage. There was a bucket with a little water in, which must have been for the rain, and a pile of leaves. Nothing else. I sighed with disappointment and started back down the ladder.

Halfway down, I felt something stab my arm, and it made me cry out. A sharp nail was sticking out from one of the beams of the tower and it had ripped my shirt and cut me. As I looked at it, I remembered that this was the nail John Winstone had mentioned.

I scrambled and slipped down the last steps as Masou and Ellie came running.

'Whatever is it, Grace?' Ellie gasped. 'Have you found something?'

'Sadly not,' I replied. 'But something has found me!' I held the candle up to my shoulder, where blood was beginning to ooze through my shirt. 'I caught myself on a nail as I came down from the tower. The shirt is torn.'

'Never mind the shirt,' said Ellie, examining the wound. 'What about you? You could get lockjaw from a scratch like that.'

'Lady Grace rendered dumb,' sighed Masou. 'What peace we would have then!'

'I could still fight you!' I reminded him, and

tried to punch him on the arm to prove it, but Masou just laughed and jumped nimbly out of the way. It is so hard to get the better of him!

'Come, we must leave,' he said. 'We have found no clues. We should make haste to the Clink.'

When we got back to the window, I insisted on climbing out first. I had decided to hide when I got down and then jump out and scare the life out of Masou, but it did not turn out as I had planned. I was just lowering myself down into the alley when I felt a strong hand grasp my jerkin. I let go of the drainpipe and dangled in the grasp of a huge, fierce-looking man who was shining a lantern in my face.

'You're coming with me, you little varmint!' the man snarled. 'Your luck's out, for I'm a jailer down at the Clink and you're trespassing on private property.' He stood me on my feet and looked me up and down. Then he gave a twisted smile which was more of a sneer. 'Of course, you could help me to forget I've seen you . . .' He paused and rubbed a finger across his palm. I knew what he meant – he wanted payment to let me go. 'But if you can't . . .'

But my brain was already awhirl. The Clink was the very place I wanted to go!

'How fortunate!' I cried. Then I remembered that I was not supposed to be speaking like a Maid of Honour. 'Er, I mean, that's lucky, innit, Mister? I was goin' there anyways. So I'll 'appily go with ya. I'm meant to be takin' vittles to my uncle. 'E's an actor at this inn. That's why I were in there. I were fetchin' 'is pipe.' I prayed he would not ask to see the pipe, for of course I had not got one!

'You have strange speech,' said the jailer, scratching his head. 'Where are you from, boy?'

I tried to think of somewhere far from Southwark. 'Hackney,' I gasped. I had no idea how they spoke in the village of Hackney, but hoped that this guard was as ignorant as me.

There was a sound above at the window and the man looked up. I held my breath. I prayed fervently that Ellie and Masou would not try to rescue me now.

'Are there more of you?' demanded the guard. 'It will go hard for you if you don't tell me straight.'

I shook my head. 'It's rats!' I told him, and he seemed satisfied. Then I saw a steely look in his eye.

'I'll take you to the Clink,' he growled. He pushed his face into mine and I could smell his foul breath. 'Only you still 'ave to pay me to let you in. Out or in, it's all the same to me. Show us your money.'

I pulled out my purse and took two coins, but the guard snatched the purse from me. Since he hadn't seen the ones in my hand, I clutched them tightly, keeping them out of sight.

'That's a lady's purse!' he exclaimed, peering inside. 'Not yours or your uncle's, I'm guessing. Still, there's just enough in there to pay. Come with me.'

I just had time to turn and look up at the window before he dragged me off. Ellie and Masou were staring open-mouthed at me, but I managed to put my finger to my lips to let them know that they were not to show themselves. On my own the guard might believe me to be a servant as I'd claimed, but if he saw that there were three of us climbing out of the window, he'd be sure to think us a band of thieves. We would all be arrested.

The jailer dragged me down the darkest, smelliest passages I have ever seen. The dark shapes of ragged people passed us, and there was raucous laughter from the grimy windows of an inn. In the distance I heard nine chimes of the clock. At last we stopped at a heavy wooden door and my captor took a large key from his belt. He opened the door and hauled me into a dark room. There was a feeble light burning in the corner and I could see a man sitting there with his feet on a table. Next to him stood a tankard of ale, a quill, an ink well and a large book.

The man swung his boots down and stood up. 'Got another one for the oven, Alf?' he said to my companion, looking at me. 'It's murderous hot in there tonight. I'll be off now you're here to take your shift.' He drained his tankard and went out into the night.

I heard his key grind as he locked the door behind him. My heart sank at the sound. There were chains with manacles hanging on the wall, waiting for the next victim, and I could hear faint groans from beyond a door in the corner. A terrible fear crept over me. Ellie was right, I thought: I should never have come to this place.

Alf motioned towards the book. ''Tis a pity you're not 'ere as a prisoner,' he said sorrowfully, 'because then I'd put your name in the book and you'd 'ave to pay me to put the chains on you. Everyone 'ere has to 'ave chains, and I don't put them on for free. My very valuable time 'as to be paid for. And then you'd 'ave to pay me to bring you food, and then, if you was found innocent, you'd 'ave to pay me to open the door again and strike the chains from your wrists. That's how it works in 'ere – the inmates pay for everything. And if they can't pay, they stay as debtors. Let that be a warning to you, boy. Now, what's your uncle's name?'

'Bartholomew Rouse,' I told him. 'Brought in today.'

Alf looked at the book. 'He's in one of the cells below.'

He pushed me down a staircase and along a corridor. I could hear groans and piteous wails. Alf stopped at one of the barred doors. While he struggled with the lock, I took the chance to slip the two coins I had been clutching into my boot. I would be needing them if I was to get out later.

As the door opened, I drew back in utter horror. The heat and a terrible stench hit me and I almost heaved. Now I knew what the guard had meant by the 'oven' – the air was so hot it was difficult to breathe. A few rush lights flickered on the walls, and I could see that the cell was crowded with dirty wretches who hardly raised their dull eyes as I was thrust inside. Some were sitting, some lying on the floor. A few looked so pale and still that they could surely not have been alive.

A few moments later

Ellie has just come to ask why I was shivering as I wrote. Did I now have a real fever? she asked, because she would not be surprised if I did, what with insisting on writing in my daybooke when I should be resting! And she would have gone on for hours like that if I had not interrupted. I had to tell her that I was merely remembering the prison and I asked her to bring me a nosegay, for I still have the stench in my nostrils.

I do not believe I can fully describe how awful it was in the Clink. I forced myself to look around me in the cell. Whatever these poor prisoners had done, they were being soundly punished for it! And that thought made me remember why I had come to the Clink – to see Bartholomew. I believed he was innocent, and I had to do everything I could to prove it. I was cross that I had let myself be distracted from my purpose. I knew I had to put the horror to one side and find him.

There was a drunken man at my feet – almost rolling over them, in fact – and I asked him (remembering to use my rough voice) if he knew of Bartholomew Rouse. Unfortunately he did not seem to understand my question, so I picked my way between the prisoners and crossed the floor, which was slippery with Heaven knows what. There were no close-stools, of course, so everyone had used the straw. I next spoke to a man who sat in a crumpled heap.

'Bartholomew Rouse?' he repeated. 'I know none but Christian names in here and I've not heard of such a one.' As I moved away, he grasped my leg with a skinny hand. 'You've just come in, haven't you, boy?' he said in a broken voice. 'You don't look wasted like the rest of us. I tell you, if you can get hold of money, buy your way out of here!'

I thanked him and glanced around the cell. How was I going to find Bartholomew amongst so many? I went on searching and asking, coming across many sights I cannot bring myself to write about. Once I tripped over an outstretched leg and a boy leaped to his feet, raising a hand to strike me. I dodged out of the way and another boy muttered that they would get me later. I hurried away from them.

I came to a group of men who had a grubby deck of cards. They had no money, but were playing for pieces of straw. I asked if they knew of Bartholomew Rouse.

'Come in today, did he?' asked one. 'There's a new prisoner over there. He was bemoaning his innocence till we told him to shut his mouth.' He gestured to a pillar behind him where someone sat, head in hands. Heavy metal bands had been clamped around his wrists and the chains were attached to a ring on the pillar.

I went over. 'Bartholomew Rouse?' I asked.

The man lifted his head. I saw hope in his eyes until he realized it was just a boy in front of him.

'Listen!' I whispered, squatting next to him. 'I am sent by Alice—'

'How is my Alice?' he interrupted eagerly. 'Tell me, boy!' He grasped my hands and winced as the iron bands cut into his flesh.

'She is well,' I said, 'and desperate to prove your innocence. But there are things you have to tell me if we are to do that. I have little time – it is not long before curfew.'

'But . . . but . . . who are you?' Bartholomew asked.

'I cannot tell you,' I said. 'But if anyone asks, say I am your nephew.'

He nodded. It was hard to be heard above the groans and shouts and clanking of chains. We were almost shouting to be heard.

'Be assured of this,' I went on: 'I have your welfare at heart. Tell me what you know of the murder of Richard Fitzgrey.'

'I know nothing,' Bartholomew replied earnestly. 'Alice and I were returning to London after our marriage, and suddenly I was clapped in irons before I even knew that Richard was dead! Richard was my friend, so why would I kill him?

But nobody will listen to me. I am doomed!'

'What do you know of Michael Fenton then?' I urged. 'Alice said you had had harsh words with him.'

'Michael Fenton,' growled Bartholomew through gritted teeth. 'I could well believe him to be the murderer.'

An argument broke out amongst the card players, and fists began to fly. I had to lean back against the pillar to avoid being hit.

'Why do you think this of Michael?' I asked Bartholomew when the fight had died down. 'Why would he want to kill Richard?'

Bartholomew frowned in concentration. 'Fenton was once hand-fasted to Alice,' he explained. 'He broke it off with her when he found a wealthier betrothed, but Richard was furious, for he had cherished high hopes that his own prospects would improve if his sister married a gentleman. Having had his hopes dashed in this respect, Richard spotted a new opportunity to make his fortune. You see, Fenton's new love did not know that he had previously been betrothed and then broken that solemn bond. Richard demanded money from Fenton to keep this secret from her and her family.'

I gasped. 'So Richard was blackmailing Michael Fenton!' I cried. At last the pieces of the puzzle were slowly starting to fit together. Blackmail was a strong motive for murder. But how was I to prove that this had happened? First I needed evidence of the blackmail.

'Richard must have had something that *proved* there had been a hand-fasting,' I said to Bartholomew. 'Something that he could make public if Fenton refused to pay. Was there a document perhaps?'

'Nothing was written,' Bartholomew replied. 'But there was a ring.' He lowered his voice and I could barely hear him. 'Michael Fenton is noble born. He gave Alice a ring with his family crest on it to seal the betrothal. Richard refused to let her give it back when the betrothal was broken. He told Fenton that he would show that ring to his new lady love. It would not have gone well with Fenton's marriage plans if it were known that he had behaved so dishonourably. But Richard told Fenton that if he paid him a large sum of money, he would keep it quiet and return the ring.'

'Did Fenton pay?' I asked.

'Yes,' replied Bartholomew gravely. 'But instead of returning the ring, Richard demanded more money. He needed the money desperately to pay off debts. He had been living too well, and tradesmen were now after him to settle up. They were becoming violent. I told him blackmail is a sin, but he wouldn't listen. We quarrelled.' Bartholomew slammed his fists down onto his knees, making his chains rattle. 'I wish I had not let poor Richard push me away,' he moaned. 'Then he might still be alive. And I would be starting my new life with Alice instead of rotting in this hellhole.'

I could not help but pity Bartholomew Rouse, only just married and now embroiled in a murder. I was determined to free him from this tragic situation if I could.

'Alice and I grew close when I was trying to help Richard with his debts,' Bartholomew continued. 'I then went to him to ask if I could wed his sister, but he said something so terrible that I knew his money troubles must have made him mad!'

'What was it?' I asked.

'I will never forget his words,' said Bartholomew sadly. 'He said, "I wish to pluck that Fenton goose a good deal yet"! And then he said that he wanted Alice to look thin and miserable to help his case — as if she were pining for her old betrothed. He told me to keep away from her, for he said I had "put a bloom on her cheeks". And then he wrote me a letter telling me our friendship was over.'

Bartholomew sighed deeply. 'Richard was not himself. Worry over his debts had sent him Bedlam. I fear he must have pushed Fenton so hard that his victim decided to rid himself of his blackmailer.'

I felt certain that Bartholomew's tale was true. For one thing he seemed to be deeply affected by what had befallen Richard, and if he was as poor an actor as everyone said, I would surely have seen through his words. But I knew that I needed evidence, for Bartholomew's story on its own would not be enough to convince Mr Hatton.

'Where is the ring now?' I asked quickly. 'It could be shown to Mr Hatton as proof of your tale.'

'Richard hid it in the casket that he held during the play,' said Bartholomew. 'Where it is now I have no idea! I fear that all hope is lost.'

But I knew where it was: safely locked with all the players' things in the storeroom at the palace! I had to find it and show it to Mr Hatton without delay.

I began to take my leave of Bartholomew, but he stopped me.

'Who are you really?' he whispered.

'A friend,' I said. 'And one who will do all he can to get you free.' I saw a faint glimmer of hope in Bartholomew's eyes as I spoke. I hated to leave him in that dreadful place, but I knew I had to go. I pushed my way through the crowded cell to the door. I heard a distant chiming of church bells but took no notice in my desperation to be out of the dreadful place. At the bars I called for the jailer.

At last he appeared, and I pulled the two coins from my boot. 'I want to leave now,' I said, holding out a sixpence and a penny. 'Here's the money!'

Alf snatched the coins and pocketed them. 'That would be enough,' he said with a horrible grin, 'if curfew hadn't just sounded. But now you'll 'ave to wait until morning – and then, o' course, I'll be wanting a night's rent.'

Of course! The bells I had heard had been chiming ten – the hour of curfew.

'But I gave you a whole purse of coins!' I shouted in desperation.

Alf took my purse out of his pocket and tossed it up and down in his hand. 'Don't remember that,' he said. 'See you at sun-up.' And he walked away, chuckling.

What was I going to do? I did not think I could bear to stay in that awful place for another minute. 'Wait!' I yelled, banging my fists on the door. 'You can't leave me here all night.'

But he had gone. How was I going to get out? I had no more money. I sank to the floor in despair.

Ellie and Masou knew where I was, yet how could they explain what I was doing in the Clink – and dressed as a boy?

I broke into a sweat of panic and felt it trickling down my face and back. The last rush light flickered and died. It was pitch black. I put my head on my knees and closed my eyes.

Unbelievably, I must have fallen asleep, for I woke with a jolt and felt something pulling at my foot.

'We'll have 'is money,' hissed a voice. ''E's got coins in that boot.'

'I'm goin' to pay 'im back for that kick in the shins,' murmured another.

With horror I realized it was the two boys I had fallen over earlier. 'Get off me!' I yelled. 'I shall tell the Queen!'

'And I'll tell me friend the Lord Mayor,' sniggered one of the curs.

Fingers were still scrabbling at my foot. The boot was tight and wouldn't give. I kicked out in the darkness.

'Want a fight, do you?' one boy growled.

'Let's turn 'im upside-down and give 'im a good shaking.'

A pair of hands grabbed me and I began to fear for my life. But then the boot gave way and I heard my other attacker fall back.

'Got it!' he muttered.

'What's in it?' asked the other.

'Not a sausage!'

'Then 'e's got 'is money hidden somewhere else.'

I swung my arms and thumped both boys hard, but felt their hands on me again. I struggled to free myself, but they were stronger than me.

Suddenly the door swung open and a shaft of lantern light fell on us. Like a flash, the boys disappeared into the dark.

'Bunting!' snarled Alf. 'Where's Bunting?'

Bunting! That was Ellie's surname. Then I saw my own damask dress marching towards me, with Ellie's head poking from it, wearing the bejewelled horsehair wig that she had used on Masou! I nearly cried with relief.

'There you are, Bunting!' shouted Ellie, wagging her finger and sounding remarkably like Lady Sarah! 'You villain! I send you out with a message for my lord and then I hear you are in the Clink visiting your no-good uncle! And a boot short! You wait until I hand you over to Mrs Fadget.' The jewels on the wig rattled as she moved, and the whole thing nearly slid off. She suddenly turned on Alf. 'How dare you detain this boy for no good reason? My husband shall hear of this – and he's a magistrate!'

Alf's jaw dropped open as Ellie squashed the wig firmly back on her head, took me by the ear and pulled me out of the cell. It did not hurt too badly, but I played my part and whimpered a little. It is a shame that Ellie is not a boy, for she would have made a fine actor.

We hastened away from the Clink – which I hope I will never cast eyes on again – and into the dark streets. Masou emerged from the darkness and I gave them both a hug.

'How wonderful to see you!' I gasped, rubbing my ear.

'You will be amazed at our cunning,' whispered Masou. 'When we realized that curfew had passed and you had not reappeared, we made haste back to the palace.'

'And I got your dress and the wig,' Ellie put in eagerly. 'And Masou got all his wages, and we came back and paid that jailer for your release. It's a good job I took such trouble dressing this wig the other day. Did you think I made a fine lady?'

'The finest,' I said, hugging them both again. My dear friends had made quite a journey on my behalf. 'And I will pay you back, Masou, I promise.'

On the way back to the river, I told my friends

all that I had learned from Bartholomew Rouse.

We reached the river stairs to find Kersey waiting patiently. 'Glad to see you got Norbert under control again.' He grinned as he pushed the boat away from the jetty. 'Strange jest you've been having in that dress, Perkin – but it's not for me to ask. I'll get you back to the palace before dawn.'

Ellie has now told me that I must put down my daybooke as I need a bath to remove the prison smells and infestations – and if I do not obey, she will fetch her husband, the magistrate!

In my chamber, an hour later

I am dressed and fragrant – and all thanks to Ellie. Mary Shelton and Lady Sarah are just having the finishing touches put to their hair, for we are off on an outing. I am taking the opportunity to write in my daybooke. Events are moving quickly and I want to have everything set down.

The minute I had put down my daybooke, the door opened and Fran and Olwen appeared, dragging a large wooden tub.

They put it by the fire, which Ellie insisted I

would need despite it being August and as hot as Hades. Kettles were boiled on the flames and even more brought in. Ellie added some musk and ambergris to the water, which smelled wonderful. Then she sprinkled the surface with rose petals.

When my tiring woman deemed the bath was warm and deep enough, I was ordered to remove my bedrobe and climb in. I thanked Fran and Olwen and they moved away.

'That's well water,' Ellie told me proudly. 'I had them draw it special. No Thames muck for you.' Fran and Olwen were attending to their mistresses' clothes and taking little notice of us, but she lowered her voice nonetheless. 'Now, Grace, you've got to back me up because I've told a fibble-fabble. Mrs Champernowne was fretting that you shouldn't go near water with a summer chill, so I sort of hinted that your uncle had suggested it as a medicinal remedy. And when we're finished, you must get dressed and show yourself before she goes to your uncle and finds it was not true.'

I nodded, and then Ellie took a rag and proceeded to scrub me all over. She did not try to be gentle and I now know how Her Majesty's little dog, Ivan, felt after he fell in the stagnant pond at Kenilworth and had to be drenched in buckets of water before he was allowed near the Queen again.

While she scrubbed, my mind went back to what I had learned last night in the Clink. I was now determined to find out all I could about Mr Fenton. He seemed a likely suspect, but I was determined to tread carefully. I'd thought the same of Bartholomew and was proved quite wrong! But if I could find real evidence that Fenton was Richard's murderer, then Bartholomew Rouse would be returned to his wife.

There was one important piece of evidence that I knew I needed: the ring with the Fenton family crest on it that Richard had used to blackmail Michael Fenton. With luck it was still where Bartholomew told me Richard had hidden it – in the jewel-encrusted treasure chest that Richard held during the play. If it was found in that chest, it would help to prove that Richard had indeed been blackmailing Michael Fenton, and likely drove him to murder.

My reasoning was all very fine, but I could not go myself to find the ring. I decided I would have to call upon Masou to climb into the storeroom again and fetch the casket.

'Can you find Masou?' I asked Ellie suddenly.

'Why so?' asked Ellie without a pause in her scrubbing. 'I'm not scrubbing him an' all!'

I laughed. 'No indeed. I wish him to climb back

into the storeroom and search for the treasure chest that Richard held in the play. Masou will know which one. I want him to see if it holds the ring that Mr Fenton gave to Alice when they were hand-fasted.'

'I saw the whole of Mr Somers's troupe not twenty minutes ago,' Ellie told me. 'They were 'eading off to the park of St James. Mr Somers wants them to practise their tumbles – with all the actors taking up the big courtyard, there's no room for them to do it there.'

Then the ring would have to wait, I thought. If it was indeed in the chest, then at least it was safely locked up until Masou was free to help.

But the ring alone would not be enough evidence to prove Mr Fenton a murderer. I needed more – another letter, perhaps, about the blackmail. I was just working out what to do next when Ellie bundled me out of the bath and into a large towel of linen. Then she sat me on a stool and took out a comb. She anointed it with a mixture of nutmeg and rosemary, mixed in some clean well water, and ran it through my hair. This was very soothing and I thought I might fall asleep, but Ellie was in a brisk mood and soon had me dressed in a fresh chemise and petticoat. She put some powder of alum under my armpits to ward off the heat and some gillyflower water on my neck and temples. By the time I was clothed in my rose gown I felt completely free of any prison taint, and I told Ellie so.

She looked me up and down with her head on one side. 'Now I will put your hair in a simple coif, because there's no time for a proper styling, more's the pity,' she sighed. Then she brightened. 'I'm sure I can put in a few trinkets.'

Ellie combed my hair back from my face according to the fashion. Then she threaded a circle of pearls into my tresses so that the front ones lay on my forehead. I peeked in the glass and it looked very well.

It was at this moment that Lady Sarah and Mary Shelton came in to see how I was faring. They told me Her Majesty was closeted in her Privy Chamber, signing state papers with Mr Secretary Cecil, so the Court had the afternoon to amuse themselves.

'Some of the young men are going to play tennis,' said Lady Sarah, 'and we are on our way to watch, but we had to see how you were first.'

I could not believe she had put *me* before the young men!

Mary Shelton took my hand. 'I am glad to see you recovered, Grace,' she said. 'I was worried about you last night. You lay so still that I thought I must call for Mrs Champernowne.'

'I just needed a long sleep,' I said quickly. 'I feel hale and hearty now.'

Lady Sarah came and inspected my hair. 'That looks comely on you, Grace,' she said, and I could tell that she truly meant it. Sometimes Lady Sarah surprises me. She turned to Ellie. 'You have some skill, Ellie Bunting,' she told her. 'Would you suggest a similar style for one with hair the colour of mine?'

I saw Ellie's cheeks flush a little. I do not think she could believe that Lady Sarah was actually asking her advice! I could see that she was enjoying this moment. 'Small pearls would look very well, my lady,' she said firmly, and nodded with the air of an expert, which made me very proud.

'Then I must buy some immediately,' declared Lady Sarah. 'For I have no strings of small pearls. Come, we shall all go to the shops!'

My heart sank. Shopping is not one of my hobbies, even if it is her favourite, and I was about to remind her of the young men playing tennis when a wonderful thought struck me. Some would say the best shops are on London Bridge, hard by St Thomas's Chapel, the home of Michael Fenton! If Lady Sarah could be persuaded to go shopping there, then I would happily go with her. Once the others had their noses in all the tempting wares, I would contrive a means of slipping away to the chapel to look for evidence of his guilt.

'Why do we not go to London Bridge then?' I suggested brightly. 'Lady Ann Courtenay would have it that the only trinkets worth putting in your hair come from Cowpers.'

'You have the right of it, Grace,' agreed Lady Sarah. She turned to Olwen. 'Quick, get me ready, and you, Fran, go and seek out Mrs Champernowne. We will need her permission to leave.'

Ellie bent down level with my ear. 'It does my heart good to hear you speak like that, Grace,' she whispered. 'I thought you would never take any pride in your appearance.'

I did not tell her my true reason for wishing to visit the bridge. She seemed so pleased that it would have been mean-spirited of me. I vowed to show a lot of interest in the trinkets on display before I took myself off to Mr Fenton's house.

Mrs Champernowne came puffing in. 'What is all this?' she panted. I believe she had forgotten the heat and rushed up the stairs. 'Are you feeling worse, Lady Grace?'

'No, madam,' I said quickly. 'I am much

recovered. A good night's rest has cured me of any ill.'

'Mrs Champernowne,' burst in Lady Sarah impatiently. 'May we visit Cowpers? I have need of some trinkets for my hair, and some netting for a new snood.'

The Mistress of the Maids considered for a moment. 'Who else will be going?' she asked.

'Why, Mary Shelton and Grace—'

'I am not sure that Grace should be going out,' huffed Mrs Champernowne. 'Not with a summer chill and after a bath.'

'But Mrs Champernowne,' I gasped before I could stop myself – surely I was not going to plan the perfect way to gain the evidence I needed and then see myself banned from going – 'I feel well; in fact, better than well!'

Mrs Champernowne came and studied me. 'Your colour is certainly good,' she said, putting a hand on my forehead. 'Hmmm, seems cool enough. But who will chaperone you? I cannot leave the palace, for Her Majesty may have need of me.'

I was pleased to hear this. As I am the youngest, it is often me that Mrs Champernowne fusses about when we are away from the palace.

'Fran and Olwen will come with us,' Lady Sarah

told her. She had taken charge, it seemed. 'I will send Fran to hire a boat for us now. May Ellie Bunting be spared? She has an eye for fashion.'

Ellie was standing behind Mrs Champernowne and I saw her beaming smile. I was delighted that she would be coming as well.

Mrs Champernowne harrumphed for a bit and then agreed. 'I saw Mr Swinburne and Sir Mark Armitage kicking their heels downstairs in the Stone Gallery. They will act as your escorts.'

Lady Sarah looked very pleased at the inclusion of Mr Swinburne in the party, until Mrs Champernowne suddenly remembered the other Maids. 'Shall I fetch Lady Jane and Carmina?' she suggested.

'Oh, we do not want to trouble them,' said Lady Sarah quickly. 'And we would need more than two escorts if there were more of us.'

Mrs Champernowne's eyes twinkled, and I do believe she was considering fetching Lady Jane just to spite Sarah, but then she relented and told us to be on our way. 'But look you are back well before supper,' was her parting shot.

Of course, we cannot be on our way immediately, for Lady Sarah now has to choose which of her twenty-seven hats she is to wear on

the trip. I have written the whole of this entry and
she is still not ready! Fie upon her!

Just after five of the clock

Mary Shelton, Lady Sarah and I have come to the
tennis courts, where the Queen and the Court are
watching some of the gentlemen play. Lady Jane
and Carmina are looking quite flushed at the sight.

'You are just in time,' whispered Carmina when
I sat down next to her on the wooden bench.
'Harry Beauchamp is playing against Mr Penshawe,
and they are very evenly matched. They have two
sets each.'

Harry Beauchamp and Mr Penshawe are both
handsome and athletic young men, if a little dim. I
could see why all the young ladies were enjoying
the spectacle. I wanted to speak with the Queen,
but she was surrounded by her retinue of ministers
and Ladies-in-Waiting and seemed engrossed in the
sport. Even the watchful Mrs Champernowne had
not noticed our return. I had guessed that I would
not find it easy to speak with Her Majesty, and so
had sent Ellie for my daybooke. I have it open on
my lap now and believe I can tear my eyes away

from the tennis to write what has occurred this
afternoon.

Our journey to London Bridge was uneventful.
The river was busy, as ever, but not too choppy, and
although we were against the tide, our boatmen
were strong. Lady Sarah enjoyed a lively
conversation with Mr Swinburne, who is a
charming young man, and Mary Shelton chatted
with Sir Mark Armitage. I was just impatient to get
to the bridge and continue my investigation.

We landed at St Mary Ovary Stairs on the south
bank and made our way along the street up onto
the bridge, passing through the Drawbridge Gate.
Sir Mark glanced up and became quite animated
about the rotting heads and quartered bodies on
the spikes, until Mary Shelton turned green.

I love London Bridge. The buildings are so
haphazard and colourful. They rear up from the
cobbles and some of the higher storeys touch as if
shaking hands. It makes a tunnel of the shops and
houses. The wooden boards, which stick out from
the shop fronts to hold the sellers' goods, are so
large that it is hard to get by them, especially in the
crowds! Today it was a hurly-burly of shouts and
smoke and snorting horses. It always surprises me
that Her Majesty does not like the bridge. She has

given no reason, but will always use a boat to cross the river even when right next to it.

Lady Sarah led us straight to Cowpers. Well, not exactly straight! Several times on the way we had to dive for the safety of a shop door to avoid the carts rumbling by. There were a crowd of people outside the shop, gathered round the long board upon which the merchandise was displayed. Overhead hung its painted sign of a needle and thread with HABERDASHERS OF SMALL WARES written underneath. One apprentice within was leaning out of the window behind the board and taking money, while another was deftly wrapping purchases up in twists of cloth. When they saw ladies of the Court, one of them sprang out of the door and bade us enter.

Lady Sarah turned to our escorts. 'Mr Swinburne and Sir Mark,' she said sweetly, 'I am sure that you gentlemen do not wish to wait upon us here, for we will be an age.'

Mr Swinburne gave a pretty speech about how he would do anything Lady Sarah commanded, but she cut him short and sent the two men off to the nearest tavern.

Inside, the apprentices called for Mr Cowper, who came and showed us all the finest things. There was a veritable treasure trove of ribbons, buttons, hair trinkets, lace and cottons. Lady Sarah and Mary Shelton rushed to each display, calling upon Fran and Olwen to look, and then turning to Ellie for her opinion as to colour and style. I stood back. It had been my idea to come on this outing, so I had to buy something, but what? I had not a clue. And I could not go in search of Mr Fenton's house on my own and without having made a purchase first. I waited for a moment, hoping to grab Ellie's attention and get her to choose something for me, but she was in her element, suggesting a pretty piece of lace for Mary Shelton, and advising against a scarlet ribbon that clashed with Lady Sarah's hair. I felt a rush of affection for her, and once again silently thanked the Queen for my friend's improved status.

Ellie held up a piece of delicate net. 'This would make a fine snood,' she announced.

'Then let us purchase the net at once and make haste for the jewellery shop,' declared Lady Sarah.

'Wait!' I said. 'I have not yet made up my mind between . . .' I grabbed the two nearest things, which turned out to be a dish of green cloth buttons that were far too rough for any of my gowns, and a paper of bone sewing needles. I looked down at them. 'You see – I need help!' I laughed. 'Why do you not go on to the jewellers? I will have Ellie help me find something and then we will join you.'

'Very well,' said Lady Sarah. 'But make haste, for I will have need of Ellie again.' And with that she made her purchase and hurried out of the door with Mary Shelton, Fran and Olwen.

'Now, Grace,' said Ellie, coming over to me and taking the buttons and needles from my hands, 'what is it that you—?'

Poor Ellie did not have time to finish, for, now that the others were safely out of the way, I grabbed her arm and rushed her from the shop. Then I scanned the busy thoroughfare.

'I might have known it,' said Ellie, rolling her eyes. 'You never wanted to shop at all, did you? You've got another mad adventure planned.'

I told her all about Fenton's house being nearby, and how I had to find more evidence to link him to Richard's murder.

'Please come with me, Ellie,' I said pleadingly. 'I can venture anywhere with you as my chaperone.'

'All right, Grace.' She grinned. 'I'm not letting you off on your own – not after you got yourself locked up in the Clink!'

We pushed through the crowds, further onto the bridge. I was mindful of pickpockets after my experience at St Paul's, and kept my purse tightly clasped under my arm. The crowds were so dense here that we were almost flattened against the shop fronts. Then there was a gap between the buildings and I had a good view of the side of the chapel house, sticking right out on a strut of the bridge, the water pounding past it and away downstream. There was not much to show that it had once been a chapel apart from its shape. I marched up to the heavy oak door and rapped the iron knocker.

Ellie caught at my arm. 'You can't go aknocking just like that,' she hissed. 'What are you going to say when someone answers?'

'I have thought of that,' I assured her. 'Do not worry.'

Ellie muttered under her breath – something about how she'd heard that before and look where it had led us – but she stopped when I gave her arm a shake.

The door was opened by a maidservant, who bowed her head when she saw me.

'Good afternoon,' I said quickly. 'My name is Lady Grace Cavendish. I am a Maid of Honour and goddaughter to Her Gracious Majesty. The Queen and I share an interest in old buildings, and this one is particularly fascinating as it is on the bridge and was once a chapel. May my tiring woman and I be admitted so that I can look around and then acquaint the Queen with what I have seen?'

The servant looked delighted. 'My master would be ever so pleased,' she gushed. 'He's that proud of the house and he's at Court often. I am sure he would want to show you round himself and I expect him back soon. If you would wait in the parlour, I will bring you some refreshment.'

'That is capital!' I declared, hoping that I sounded convincing. I wanted to search for clues if I could, and that would be difficult with Mr Fenton in attendance. 'However, I do have to be back at Whitehall Palace before the tide turns. Could you show me the house while we wait for him? I am so fascinated by it.'

The servant, who was called Bessie, ushered us in eagerly and we began our tour. The house was indeed narrow but very deep. We could hear the constant rush of the water as it flowed between the arches.

'That never stops,' said Bessie, 'but you get used to it. It lulls me off to sleep of a night, though I've heard of some that couldn't stand it and had to move.' She led us up some winding steps. 'This was a chapel in the days of King Henry,' she went on, 'but since then it's been all sorts until Sir George Fenton made it into a home. It were a grocer's at one time and I swear you can still smell the spices in the basement.'

We had now reached a parlour on the second floor. There were many mullioned windows and the little diamond-shaped panes sparkled in the sunlight. I tried to look for clues without being too obvious.

Ellie gazed out over the river. 'It's like being on a big ship!' she breathed.

''Tis that,' chuckled Bessie. 'And if you look over there, you can see the moat at the Tower.'

I made some appreciative noises and we were led down to the next storey. Here was a room obviously used as a study. There was a desk with papers scattered all about. I quickly glanced at the top documents, but of course there were no blackmail letters there. If only I could have sifted through at my leisure. But we did not linger, much to my disappointment.

Now Bessie led us down to the kitchen, which was built directly over the pier. Another servant was stirring a big steaming vat of soapy water.

'If you don't mind being down here with us folk,' said Bessie shyly, 'the best view of all is from the kitchen window. You can see the boats that have chanced it and shot the bridge! They come out like corks from a bottle. 'Tis most comical. I'm sure you've heard the saying, "Wise men walk over London Bridge while only fools go under it." '

Ellie went straight to have a look. As much as I would have liked to see the view, I realized that here was my chance to slip back to the study if I just pretended that I had dropped something up there. I was just backing to the door when Ellie turned to speak to me. She was smiling, but suddenly her face changed.

'No!' she yelled.

We all jumped. Ellie rushed over to the steaming vat and wrested a piece of dripping material from the puzzled servant. It must have been hot, but Ellie did not notice. She is used to such things from her time in the Queen's laundry, I suppose.

'You never put stains like that in hot water!' she admonished the servant. 'That's blood, that is,' she said, pointing to a brown mark on what seemed to be a white linen shirt. 'Blood *sets* in hot water. You'll never get it out now.'

Bessie came over and looked at the shirt. 'You birdbrain, Ruth,' she scolded. 'You know Master was most particular about having this shirt cleaned. He is careful with his money and don't like to buy new if old can be restored.'

I peered over Ellie's shoulder at the ruined shirt. The bloodstain was at the top of the left sleeve and there was a tear in the fabric as well. How had that happened? As if in answer to my question, I felt a tingle in my own left arm, just where I had scratched it when I climbed down from the tower on the players' stage. I had found the clue for which I had been searching! This would show that Mr Fenton had climbed up the tower on the day of the play — when the nail had been sticking out — wearing this very shirt. But I remembered that no one had seen him in the Key Inn. Perhaps he had been in disguise, I thought.

'Is this indeed your master's shirt?' I asked, for all my surmising would be for nothing if it were not.

'Yes.' Bessie nodded glumly.

I wanted that shirt; it was evidence. I had to think quickly. 'Then it is my fault that it is now spoiled,' I said. 'I insisted upon this tour and distracted poor Ruth.' I delved into my purse and produced some coins. 'I will pay for you to buy a new shirt, and I'll take this one for my groom. Ellie can mend the tear and he will be glad of it. Your master need never know.'

Bessie and the hapless Ruth goggled at me for a few moments.

'That is kind of you, I'm sure,' Bessie said at last.

'I am quite decided upon it,' I said firmly. 'And now, if we are to catch the tide . . .' I made for the passage. It was time to get this shirt back to Whitehall and tell the Queen my suspicions, and I did not particularly want to meet Michael Fenton on the way. Ellie took the shirt, wrung it out hard and rolled it up. We took the stairs that led to the front door. At that moment it opened and a tall, dark-haired man strode into the house. Ellie just had time to thrust the shirt behind her back.

'Oh, sir!' poor Bessie cried, somewhat flummoxed by the sight of her master.

He looked equally surprised to see a lady and her servant in his home. There was only one thing for it. I had to be bold.

I stepped forward. 'Mr Fenton?' I asked. My heart was beating hard, but I spoke in a voice as pleasant as I could muster, bearing in mind that I believed this fellow to be a murderer! 'I am Lady Grace Cavendish, Maid of Honour and goddaughter to the Queen.'

He swept me a very pretty bow. 'I am deeply honoured,' he said, 'but a little puzzled to find you in my humble house.'

'You must forgive me for being nosy,' I told him. 'I saw your house, remembered it had once been a chapel, and wished to see inside.'

'I was just going to offer the ladies some refreshment,' Bessie said nervously.

'Then we will go to the parlour,' said Mr Fenton, holding his hand out to indicate that we should precede him up the stairs to that room.

Ellie and I had no choice but to go. Ellie sidled past him, keeping her hands and the shirt behind her back. I wondered what was going on in Michael Fenton's mind. I think he was keen to show hospitality to someone as close to the Queen as I was. He excused himself, saying that he would just wash the street off his hands.

Ellie and I sat in the parlour. Bessie brought some cheap-tasting white wine and a dish of apricots. The fruit was somewhat overripe, but she pressed them on us anyway and Ellie took several.

'Ellie!' I said, shocked at her lack of manners.

'I'm grateful that she takes them,' laughed Bessie. 'We have an abundance. My master, who can't abide them, ordered me to get a huge basketful. I don't know what he wanted them for. He took some of them off the other day, but there's a heap of them left, and Ruth and I can't eat them all.'

Something stirred at the back of my mind when she said this. I felt it was important, but at that point Mr Fenton returned and interrupted my thoughts.

'Forgive me, Lady Grace,' he said, looking at me quizzically, 'but I still find it surprising that you would visit just to see the house. There is little of the chapel about it now.'

I saw that I needed a better excuse, and racked my brains for something that Michael Fenton might find convincing. Hell's teeth! He would be sure to start suspecting my motives if I could not come up with something plausible. 'I could not speak freely in front of your servant, Mr Fenton,' I said at last in a hushed tone. At this, Ellie seemed to get the hint and went to stare out of the window. I wondered briefly where she had put the shirt, but brushed that aside as I had to go on with my tale. 'I have news for you,' I went on, thinking furiously. 'You see . . . my, er, Great-aunt Frances – on the Cavendish side – has just died. She lived in far off, er, Cumberland, and there is some . . . well . . . dispute about her inheritance.'

Mr Fenton tried to look interested, but I am sure he was wondering what this had to do with him. I had to elaborate, so I tried to remember what Mary Shelton had once told me about a similar matter in her family.

'Apparently she is also a distant relative of yours, Mr Fenton,' I continued. He looked interested at this and I was encouraged. 'There are two wills,' I told him. 'One of them names you and me as the beneficiaries. I believe you are a second cousin . . .

though distant?' My host nodded eagerly. 'And the other document names some relatives of whom I have never heard. The inheritance needs to be distributed, but the lawyers are trying to decide to whom it should go.'

I had no idea how this story was going to be received. It sounded rather lame as I told it, and I hoped that Mr Fenton would not ask me any legal questions. But I had bargained well on the man's greed and thirst for advancement.

'Dear . . . Aunt . . . Frances,' he stuttered, closing his eyes as if remembering the past. 'I remember her well. It took us days to journey to Cumberland, but I was always glad to go. She told me such stories!'

I nodded gravely. Great-aunt Frances existed only in my fictional tale, but now Mr Fenton was bringing her to life.

'I will do anything the lawyers ask,' he was saying, leaning forward. 'An inheritance, you say?'

Bessie came in with some more apricots. She did not offer them to her master, of course, and it was then that I realized what had been bothering me about the apricots. More pieces of the puzzle were falling into place. I had seen a fruit seller's tray of apricots discarded beside the tower in the Key Inn, and at the play Masou had joked about the apricot seller having a hairy face. Had Mr Fenton ordered apricots, even though he did not like them himself, so that he could go to the play disguised as an apricot seller?

Of course, he knew nothing of my thoughts and was still in full flow about the aunt I had invented. 'She always said that I was her favourite nephew,' he reminisced, 'and that she would remember my kindness to her in her will . . .'

I nodded, but scarcely heeded him. I was picturing the scene at the inn. If my suspicions were correct, then, when Richard was in the middle of his speech, Mr Fenton had crept along to the tower, discarded his unwanted apricots and his cloak, climbed the ladder and fired the arrow that had killed Richard Fitzgrey. Then he had climbed down again – tearing his shoulder on the nail – covered himself in his cloak once more, and hurried away from the inn moments before the crime was discovered. He had not thought his shirt would give him away and so he had tossed it into a pile of laundry for washing and mending. I now had the whole story, and evidence, to lay before the Queen and Mr Hatton. I just hoped that they would be convinced.

'You will speak up for me in this dispute, will you not, Lady Grace?' Mr Fenton asked earnestly.

'I, in my turn, will speak up for you, and together we will have what is rightfully ours.'

I stood up. I wished to return to the palace and get away from this horrible man. If he was indeed the murderer, I sincerely hoped that he *would* get what was rightfully his! 'I will write to you further on this matter,' I told him. 'But now I fear the tide will soon turn and the Queen is expecting me back at Whitehall.' And Ellie and I made our exit as quickly as we could.

Out in the street again, Ellie and I hurried along to the jewellery shop. On the way I bought a linen bag big enough to put the shirt in. I wondered how we were going to explain our absence to the other Maids. But Lady Sarah and Mary Shelton were engrossed in choosing some seed pearls and did not seem to have noticed the time. As soon as Lady Sarah saw Ellie, she took her arm and dragged her over to the counter. Ellie just had time to thrust the damp linen bag and its contents into my hands.

'I like the look of these small ruby clips,' said Lady Sarah. 'Do you think they would look well in my hair?'

Ellie soon steered her away from the rubies that would have clashed with her copper locks, and had her purchasing an emerald clip instead.

'It compliments your hair and your beautiful skin tone,' said Ellie.

Lady Sarah was delighted, and I could see that Ellie was right. She truly is the best tiring woman ever.

I believe the tennis is drawing to a close and I can have speech with the Queen at last. I have Michael Fenton's shirt with me in the linen bag and it is making a huge damp patch on my skirt! It would have been so much easier if I had had Her Majesty's direction to investigate this mystery, but there it is.

Eight of the clock, before supper

We should be at supper now, but it has been delayed after the events of this afternoon! Such a lot has happened that I have escaped to the herb garden to write it all down while it is still fresh in my mind. The other Maids are still dressing. Lady Sarah will be an age. Unfortunately for us, she left London Bridge with a choice of jewelled clips and cannot decide which to wear in her hair. The day is cooler now that the sun is going down and I am surrounded by the lovely smells of lavender and thyme. Perfect peace after the excitement of the day!

When, at long last, the tennis finished, I scurried over to the Queen, dodging the groups of courtiers who were standing around discussing the result. I was a little breathless by the time I reached her, and she raised an eyebrow as I tripped and fell into a clumsy curtsy at her feet.

'Thank you for *Grace-ing* us so delicately with your presence, my lady,' said Her Majesty dryly, and those around her laughed as people always do, whether or not the royal joke is funny. Then she nodded for me to speak.

'My Liege,' I puffed as I struggled to disentangle my slippers from the hem of my petticoats. 'I beg a private word with you on a matter of great' – I hesitated, for I could not say anything in front of all these people that would suggest my involvement in the mystery – 'on an *intrigue* of mine,' I finished. I prayed that she would understand the message.

Her Majesty said nothing and looked rather stern. If my mission had not been so important, my heart would have failed me at her disapproval. 'A puzzle for me, Lady Grace?' she said at last and beckoned to me to accompany her. I followed her to the shade of an oak tree out of earshot of the rest of the Court.

'Well, Lady Grace?' she said with some
impatience. 'I hope that the intrigue is worth it, for
you have taken me from a most interesting
conversation with the Saxon Ambassador.'

I knelt, this time hitching up my skirts, and took
a deep breath. 'Your Majesty, I know who
murdered Richard Fitzgrey,' I said simply. 'It is—'

'So do we all, Grace,' the Queen interrupted,
narrowing her eyes, 'and he is safely locked up in
the Clink. Why do you waste my time and your
breath on old news? Be gone with you!' She waved
her fan crossly to dismiss me.

'But Bartholomew Rouse is not the murderer!' I
insisted. 'I believe it to be Michael Fenton. And
there is evidence!' I realized with horror that I
should not have spoken so directly to the Queen.

'Methinks sometimes you take your duties too
far, madam!' said the Queen slowly. 'Mr Hatton has
found the culprit, just as I assured you he would,
and yet you have decided to meddle – though I
told you that you need not concern yourself with
this matter!'

Now I was desperate. Somehow I had to make
Her Majesty listen to me.

'I beg you to hear my tale, My Liege,' I said,
almost in tears. 'Would not Your Majesty be most

angry to hear that an innocent man had been sent to the gallows? A man with a young bride whose heart would surely break at the news?'

The Queen looked at me for a long moment. 'I see you are sincere, my goddaughter,' she said in a softer tone. 'Rise then, and we shall go to my Privy Chamber. There I will listen.'

The Queen led the Court back into the palace. With every step I was praying that she would not change her mind before I could explain. But we reached the Privy Chamber at last.

Once the door had been closed behind us, I told her all about Michael Fenton's previous engagement to Alice, Richard Fitzgrey's decision to blackmail Mr Fenton with the ring, and, of course, Bartholomew's marriage, which the priest would verify had been taking place at the time of the murder.

'This is a grave charge,' said Her Majesty slowly when I had finished. I held my breath, waiting to see what she would do. 'I think I must trust the judgement of my Lady Pursuivant, since it has been proved good so often in the past,' she went on, and I felt dizzy with relief at her words.

'I remember Michael Fenton for his frequent and irritating pleas for a position at Court,' the Queen continued thoughtfully. 'Yet, though he *is* tedious, if Mr Hatton is to confront him with a charge of murder, you must furnish us with strong evidence. Have you any?'

I produced the damp shirt from the bag and showed her the tear and the bloodstain. Then I told the Queen all about the nail in the tower. I said I had overheard the player, John Winstone, talking about it when I was walking her dogs, which was true in a way.

The Queen inspected the shirt. Luckily she did not ask how I came by it. 'This alone is not proof enough, I fear,' she said. 'There are many ways to rip a sleeve. We need the ring that Michael Fenton gave to Alice on their betrothal – and proof that it was in Richard Fitzgrey's possession.'

'I believe I know where that is, Your Majesty!' I cried in excitement. 'In the Silverland chest that you yourself saw Richard carry in the play.'

The Queen immediately called for a guard to fetch the chest and he soon returned and put it on the table. I wonder if he thought it strange that the Queen of England should send for a simple wooden players' box!

When the guard had withdrawn, Her Majesty flung open the chest. It was completely empty! My heart sank. Where was the evidence I so desperately needed? Then it occurred to me that the ring had been very precious to Richard, so he would have been likely to hide it where no one would stumble upon it. Bartholomew had said it was in the chest, so perchance the chest contained a hiding place.

'Your Majesty, may I have your permission to look inside?' I asked.

'Much good may it do you, Grace,' said the Queen, pushing the casket towards me. 'I think we can go no further with this.'

I was not going to give up. I took the box and examined it. It was finely carved, and although the jewels could not have been precious stones, their colours gave a grand effect. I was hoping to find a secret compartment in the bottom, but I could soon tell that the base was far too shallow to conceal anything. The sides were of thin wood too. That only left the lid, which was slightly padded with a rough red cloth that I remembered had looked like rich velvet when we watched the play. I felt all round it. There did not seem to be anything unusual there either.

'I think you must give it up, Grace,' the Queen said gently. 'There is nothing there.'

I began to think that she was right. Perhaps Bartholomew had been mistaken. Or perhaps Richard moved the ring after he had fallen out with him. I feared that Michael Fenton was going to get away with his crime, and poor Bartholomew Rouse was going to pay—

But then my fingers felt something strange. 'Oh!' I exclaimed, and the Queen leaned forward to watch.

There was a short line of stitching where the cloth was joined to the wooden lid with nails. I started to pick away at it, and at last found an end to pull. The material puckered up as I drew the thread out. It left a small hole in the lining. I slid my fingers into it and felt around until I touched something hard and smooth and round. It was a ring!

Nervously I hooked my finger round it and drew it out. It was a very fine ring, made of gold that glinted and gleamed in the light. I peered at it eagerly, and to my delight saw that the Fenton family crest was clearly engraved upon it. This was the ring that Richard had used to blackmail Michael Fenton!

I held it out to the Queen. She took it, examined the crest, and immediately called for a page to fetch Mr Hatton.

And then everything happened very quickly. Before I knew it, Mr Fenton had been commanded to appear before the Queen, and the whole Court was assembled in the Great Hall – with the players too. It was a squeeze and there was a buzz of excitement as everyone murmured to each other, wondering what was going on.

The courtiers looked puzzled, the players fearful. Her Majesty sat stiffly upright on her high-backed chair and I could see that she was bristling with fury. Mr Secretary Cecil and her other ministers were standing around her, and I stood with the other Maids at her side. I spotted Masou amongst the throng and was bursting to tell him what had happened, but had to satisfy myself that he would know very soon. Faced with the evidence against him, I was sure that Mr Fenton would admit his crime at once.

The guards flung open the great wooden doors and Michael Fenton walked in. But 'walked' is the wrong word, for he *strutted*. He wore a fine doublet of pure silk, brown calfskin boots and a velvet cloak. He must have borrowed heavily on his upcoming marriage to afford such finery, and as his servants had told me that he usually spent as little as possible, I imagined he would only wear it when he really needed to impress. His fiancée, Catherine Lloyd, followed him in, on the arm of her father. Mr Fenton must have brought them along, hoping to impress them with the fact that the Queen herself had demanded his presence. He was in such a high mood he failed to notice that he was flanked by four grim Gentlemen of the Guard. He caught sight of me and nodded – of course, he believed me to be a distant cousin.

He swept into an over-elaborate bow and knelt before the Queen.

'A most well-mannered young man I see before me,' said Her Majesty coldly.

Mr Fenton began to simper as if he were going to be given a knighthood! 'I am ever your loyal servant, My Liege . . .'

'But not so loyal as to stop you from committing the murder of Richard Fitzgrey!' the Queen rapped out, and a gasp of shock ran round the Great Hall. Catherine Lloyd turned pale. 'What have you to say for yourself, sir?'

Mr Fenton looked astounded. 'Your Majesty, I am no murderer! What reason would I have? I did not even know Richard Fitzgrey. I never met him.'

'Fitzgrey was blackmailing you,' said the Queen. 'A large sum of money was found on his body. Money which you had given him to ensure that he did not reveal a certain secret of yours.'

'But I have no secrets, o Gracious Majesty,' Mr Fenton insisted calmly, 'as anyone who knows me will testify.' He sounded so sincere that I was almost beginning to believe him myself!

'If you are innocent, you will have no objection to satisfying my curiosity on one or two matters,' said the Queen smoothly.

'I am at your command, My Liege,' gushed Mr Fenton, bowing deeply.

'Do you know of a Mistress Alice?' she asked.

'The name means nothing to me,' replied Mr Fenton, but I thought I glimpsed a flicker of worry in his eyes.

'How strange,' said the Queen, 'for she claims to know you rather well. Indeed, she says that you and she were hand-fasted – until you broke that solemn bond.'

I saw Catherine stagger and clutch her father's arm. Mr Lloyd looked daggers at his future son-in-law.

'Your Majesty,' said Fenton, as if considering the matter, 'I think I have remembered the woman of whom you speak. The poor wretch was enamoured of me from afar and must have dreamed up this tale to discredit me. It would not be the first time a handsome man has attracted attention without his knowledge.'

I wanted to scream and shake the truth out him.

'Enough of this arrogance!' The Queen motioned to a guard, who handed her the ring. She held it out towards Michael Fenton. I saw a faint flush of colour come over his cheeks as he saw it.

'Here is the very ring you gave to Alice as a sign of your betrothal,' she said. 'Now how will you defend yourself?'

Yes, Mr Fenton, I thought to myself. You cannot deny this. We have you!

But Michael Fenton merely smiled. 'Why, that ring was stolen from my house some months since, Your Majesty. I humbly thank you. I am glad to have it back. I see now who must have taken it. It was that sad young woman, Alice. She has proved to be a liar *and* a thief.'

'Indeed.' The Queen nodded. Then, swift as a striking adder, she snapped out another question. 'What do you know of the exposed nail in the players' weather tower?'

The question took Mr Fenton completely by surprise, and for the first time he looked afraid. 'I kn-know nothing of it, My Liege,' he stammered. 'Nothing at all.'

'Then we will ask someone who can remind you,' said the Queen. 'Where is John Winstone? Step forward, man.'

Cap in shaking hands, John stepped out from among the players and fell to his knees in front of her.

'John Winstone is one of the troupe who performed *Intrigue* on that fateful day, Mr Fenton,' Her Majesty explained. 'He knows all about the nail in the tower. Rise and tell us now, John, so that all can hear!'

'Yes, indeed, Your Gracious Majesty,' said John. 'The weather towers were built on the morning of the play, and a nail was left sticking out. I were caught by it and it has made such a mark as will scar badly, I warrant. I were going to knock it in when we heard word that Your Majesty would grace us with your royal presence.' Here he bowed and his voice became stronger. He was warming to his role. 'Well, it went right from my head – we were all that excited and eager to be ready!' He stopped and blushed with horror. 'My Liege,' he mumbled, 'in no way did I mean to blame Your Royal Majesty for causing me to forget – it was just that—'

'Peace, John,' said the Queen kindly. 'I take no insult from what you say – and I think you have done me a great service by leaving the nail sticking out.'

John looked most relieved. 'Now, Your Majesty, that's not to say I would usually leave a nail sticking out. Why, I am the first to—'

'Which shoulder bears the mark of the nail?' the

Queen broke in.

'My right,' said John, a little crestfallen that she did not want to hear about his devotion to duty.

'Get to your feet, Michael Fenton,' ordered Her Majesty, 'and bare your right arm.'

I was astonished to see that Mr Fenton looked quite calm as he stood up. Surely he was about to reveal the cut that would convict him of murder! I could not understand it. Was he mad? I wondered.

Two Gentlemen of the Guard stepped up to Fenton and unlaced the sleeve of his doublet. Then, smiling all the time, he slowly rolled up the sleeve of his shirt and bared his arm. There was not a mark upon it.

'I have done protesting my innocence, Your Majesty,' he cried, striking his shoulder. 'This proves it for me without words. I have been wrongly accused of murder and I demand justice. My good name must be restored!' He began to call down curses upon whoever had made the accusations against him. Then he caught my eye and I remembered with horror that he thought I was his cousin and would jump to his defence! I quickly looked away as two of Her Majesty's advisers took him aside to try and calm him down.

The Queen sat as still as a statue, her lips thin and tight. Murmurs went round the Court. I imagine everyone was wondering what would happen now. I was as confused as everybody else. I knew Fenton had gashed his shoulder on that nail just as surely as I had, and yet there was no sign of a wound!

I put my hand to my own shoulder as I remembered how it had hurt. And suddenly I realized what had happened. The cut from the nail was on my *left* shoulder, not my right. And the bloodstain on the shirt was also on the *left* sleeve, so Michael Fenton's wound must be on his *left* shoulder. No wonder he had been so calm when told to bare his right arm! Now I recalled John Winstone's words when I had first spoken to him about the nail. 'I'm always muddling my left and right,' he had said. He had done it again just now – and what a time to do it!

I stepped up to the Queen's chair, though I do not know how I dared, for she looked so stern. 'Please would Your Majesty ask John Winstone to raise his right hand?' I whispered.

'What fresh nonsense is this, Grace?' hissed the Queen. 'Thanks to you I have already made false accusation against an innocent man – albeit an odious one – and now you would have me play nursery games!'

'I pray you, indulge me, My Liege,' I begged in a

low tone. 'Michael Fenton may be guilty yet. John does not know his left from his right!'

The Queen understood immediately. She stood and we all fell silent. 'John Winstone, raise your right hand,' she commanded.

A worried frown creased John's brow. 'I beg Your Majesty's forgiveness if I get it wrong,' he said, 'for I do have such trouble remembering which is which.' He looked from one hand to the other and at last raised his left hand.

'Thank you, John,' said the Queen, smiling. 'And is that the same side that was scratched by the nail?' John nodded eagerly. A murmur of interest went round the Court as some grasped the meaning of this. Her Majesty gestured towards the players. 'Return to your friends, John Winstone. Your duty here is done.' Then her tone changed. 'But there is one gentleman here with whom I have not finished. Michael Fenton, stand forward!'

Mr Fenton did so, for all the world as if he were waiting for an apology from Her Majesty!

'Bare your left arm,' the Queen commanded.

Mr Fenton's face went ashen. 'Your Majesty, I protest. I have been wrongly accused; am I now to be humiliated as well?'

At a signal from the Queen, two Gentlemen of the Guard marched up and held him firmly. Mr

Hatton tore out the lace from his sleeve. Fenton struggled and growled like a rabid dog, but he was no match for his captors. Mr Hatton pulled up Mr Fenton's shirtsleeve – and revealed a vivid red gash on the skin!

'My Liege,' spluttered Mr Fenton, 'I am innocent! This was done in a sword fight three days since—'

'Silence, cur!' shouted the Queen. 'You will give me the truth about the murder of Richard Fitzgrey!'

'I tell you, I know nothing . . .' whimpered Michael Fenton.

Her Majesty motioned to a servant, who brought forward the shirt with its rip and bloodstain. 'This is yours, I believe,' she told Mr Fenton curtly, 'found at your home this very day.'

Mr Fenton looked around desperately, as if seeking a way to escape, but he was hemmed in by guards and courtiers. He looked once more at the Queen and then threw himself to the floor.

'Have mercy on me,' he cried. 'I did kill Richard Fitzgrey, but the miserable dog deserved it!'

Everyone gasped. There was a scuffle near me as Mr Lloyd lunged forwards to attack Michael Fenton but was stopped by Mr Hatton.

'Look to your daughter,' Mr Hatton hissed. And,

indeed, poor Catherine had fallen into a deep faint at hearing of the villainy of her fiancé.

Now Mr Fenton had a look of cold defiance on his face. 'Fitzgrey wanted money before he would return the ring I gave his sister. Yes, we were hand-fasted but it meant nothing. She was too lowly for me.' I heard angry muttering amongst the players at this. 'I paid him what he demanded, but he was not content with that and threatened to tell my new betrothed's father about Alice if I did not give him more. My engagement would have been over and I could not have that. I deserve to marry into wealth. So I disguised myself as an apricot seller, went to the inn with my bow and arrows and waited my chance.'

I could not believe what I was hearing. Fenton was boasting about how he had committed the murder.

'Of course, the Court arriving was a diversion I could have done without,' he spat. 'But then I saw the tower. I climbed up there and waited for the final act. Players blab and I knew about the death scene. It was simple to shoot an arrow into Richard's wicked heart. I had to. He would have bled me dry if I had not put an end to him! As a gentleman, I felt it was my duty to rid the place of a man like him! Fitzgrey was the evil doer, not me.

I had to stop his mouth before he blackened the name of my noble family.'

'*You* have blackened your family's name without any help from Richard Fitzgrey,' declared the Queen grimly. 'Your desperate scrambling after wealth and nobility has ruined the name of Fenton and sunk you lower than any player. Guards, take this worthless wretch from my sight! And make sure that Bartholomew Rouse is released forthwith.'

Mr Hatton and his men dealt with Michael Fenton swiftly, as if removing rubbish from Her Majesty's presence.

'He will be hanged,' whispered Mary Shelton to me.

The Queen spoke quietly with Mr Secretary Cecil and Mr Hatton. Then she turned to address us.

'I give you all leave to depart,' she said, 'but first a few matters. Catherine Lloyd, you may stay at Court and we will find a more suitable husband for you. And where is Mr Alleyn?' The leader of the players came forward, bent at the waist. 'I wish to see the rest of your play, sir,' she said kindly. 'In the midst of all this murder and deceit we had forgot that there is still the intrigue of your play to unravel. Be sure to have it set up for the morrow in the Tilting Yard. My Court stands in sore need of something to entertain and intrigue.'

And with that we all bowed and made to leave. 'Wait, Lady Grace,' called the Queen. 'I have a matter to discuss with you.'

When all was quiet, she looked at me closely. 'How came you by all this information, my Lady Pursuivant?' she asked.

I thought of how I had got Masou to break into the storeroom, and of my trips to London Bridge and the dreadful Clink. I could never tell Her Majesty any of that. 'I listened to some talk,' I said.

The Queen smiled. 'Then your ears must be quite worn out from all that listening,' she said. 'I know how to remedy that. You must have some new earrings. I think a gold cross topped by a single pearl would refresh those poor ears.'

*The Fifteenth Day of August, in the Year of
Our Lord 1570*

It is late afternoon and the Tilting Yard is now quiet
after the afternoon's activities so I have come here to
write in my daybooke. We have a happy ending to
the tumult of the last few days . . .

The Queen announced at breakfast that she
would see the play at three of the clock. Mr Somers's
troupe and the players must have been hard pressed
but they managed to erect a stage with side wings,
hidden from the audience by painted trees. There
were no towers this time, I was glad to see, but I did
wonder how they would contrive the storm scene.

We took our places in the Tilting Yard. The Court
filled the stand, with the Queen in her usual seat, and
I was pleased to see that all the servants had been
allowed to come and stand around the edge of the
yard. I took a place beside the Queen, with Mary
Shelton on my other side. I saw Bartholomew, now
released from the Clink, standing amongst the
servants with his arm lovingly around Alice. Then I
saw Ellie. She was near the front of the crowd and
would have a wonderful view. The Queen bent

her head to me and, in a loud, carrying voice, told me that my hair had never looked better.

'Your tiring woman is doing you proud, Lady Grace,' she said.

I caught Ellie's eye. She had obviously heard every word, as I believe the Queen intended, and looked flushed and delighted. I do not think Her Majesty could have thought of a better gift. I scanned the crowds for Masou but I could not see him anywhere. He was not with the troupe or the young men of the Court. I hoped he had a good view, but I had no time to think on it any longer as the play was about to begin.

Mr Alleyn began his introduction as before, but there had been a change to the words. 'Let me transport you to the mythical kingdom of Silverland. In Silverland lived a Moor, the Count William . . . the richest man in all the realm.'

We did not have to puzzle long about the change in the words, for onto the stage stepped Masou! He was playing the lead role and his brown skin fitted the role of Moor perfectly.

I was gladdened to see that my friend John had kept his place in the play and he did very well. Then I gave my mind to the intrigue, since that is what we were there for, after all. We saw the three enemies trying to kill William the Moor and meeting their own ends instead.

Suddenly it struck me that the green enemy was supposed to be an accomplished swordsman and yet had tripped and fallen on his own sword. Were we meant to think that he had faked his death so that he could hide and shoot the arrow at Count William? But I decided that it was too obvious a solution, designed to lead the spectators down that path and thus distract them from the true murderer. Then I thought about how William's other enemies had died. The blue enemy had meant to poison William, but had drunk the fatal brew himself. That death seemed clear, for William was alive, which meant that the blue enemy must have drunk from the poisoned cup. But what of the red enemy? He had made a huge show of drowning, taking his poor servant with him. Had he truly died? We had seen a body wrapped in his cloak, but it was not necessarily *his* body! I felt certain that he must be the murderer. I leaned over and whispered to Her Majesty so that she could be the one to solve the intrigue.

We were coming to the part of the play where William was shot. It had gone so wrong before, and now it was my dear friend, Masou, who stood waiting for the arrow. Was he wearing padding? Who was in charge of the bow? I covered my face with my hands.

'Do not worry, Grace,' the Queen murmured in a low voice. 'Master Masou has doubled the padding and Cyril the bowman is taking his normal role. He always shot true before.'

Even so I had to watch from between my fingers. The fatal arrow flew through the air and Masou fell to the stage. He lay there motionless, eyes staring up at the sky as the blood spurted from his doublet. Then I saw it. It was so fast that I nearly missed it. Masou winked! And I could enjoy the spectacle once more.

Mr Alleyn gave his powerful speech about who could have killed this heroic Moor. When he had finished, there was much muttering amongst the Court as people tried to work it out. Then the Queen stood up.

'It was a fine play and splendidly acted,' she declared. I felt a burst of pride for Masou, for he had been very good. Everyone clapped and cheered. Then the Queen held up her hand for silence. 'And I believe that I have solved the mystery,' she went on. 'Mr Alleyn, you have spun a tangled web for our delight! One enemy drowned, one poisoned by his own hand and one run through with his own sword. I think a false trail has been laid to give us two suspects.' The Queen smiled round at the audience. She was enjoying herself. 'The blue enemy drank poison and there is no doubt that he died. However, the enemy in green was an expert with the sword, so his clumsy death was sure to arouse our suspicions.'

Some of the audience nodded in agreement. I heard Sir Pelham say that he had known it was the green enemy all along.

'Yet I do not believe that he was the murderer,' continued the Queen.

There was a hushed silence, during which Sir Pelham whispered that nor did he.

'We saw the enemy in red drowned with his servant. Or did we? A body in a red cloak was pulled from the water. But did not William remind us that drowning distorts the face so that it no longer resembles its living self? This drowned face did not – because it was *not* the red enemy's face, but that of his servant! The enemy in red survived, found his servant's body and put his own cloak around it. I declare that the red enemy is therefore the murderer!'

Mr Alleyn bowed deeply. 'You have solved our mystery, My Liege,' he said. 'We have performed this play a hundred times and no one else had the wit to see the intrigue.'

The Tilting Yard erupted as everyone stood and clapped Her Majesty. She stood beaming and waving at us all. Mr Alleyn left the stage, fell onto one knee and held out the purse of silver.

The Queen took it. 'I thank you,' she said. Then she motioned to Mr Cecil, who placed a similar purse in her hand. She held this out to Mr Alleyn. 'It is my wish that the players be duly compensated for all their trouble in performing this play for me and my Court.'

'She will have given them the same amount, if not a little more,' whispered Mary Shelton. 'They will not have lost money today.'

The Queen sat down and leaned towards me. 'There, Grace,' she whispered merrily. 'Such puzzles are soon solved if you merely listen to some talk!' And we both burst out laughing, to the surprise of those around us.

Under the cover of her skirts, Her Majesty took my hand and squeezed it. This was her way of thanking me for solving the two intrigues and it made me glow all over. Being a Maid of Honour to Her Majesty may involve much listening to tedious speeches, and learning of Latin and fussing over attire, but as long as there are mysteries to solve for the Queen, I am most happy to be at Court. Indeed, I can hardly wait to find a new intrigue to investigate. Something tells me it will not be long in coming . . .

GLOSSARY

addle-pated – muddle-headed

aiglet – the metal tip of a lace, which you thread through the hole

ambergris – a waxy substance made by sperm whales and found floating in the sea. It was used in perfume

Bedlam – the major asylum for the insane in London during Elizabethan times – the name came from Bethlem Hospital

Board of Green Cloth – the main administrative body for the Court. It dealt with an inquest if anyone died within one mile of the Queen's person

bodice – the top part of a woman's dress

casket – a small decorative box

chemise – a loose shirt-like undergarment

close-stool – a portable toilet comprising of a seat with a hole in it on top of a box with a chamber pot inside

Cloth of Estate – a kind of awning which went over the Queen's chair to indicate that she was the Queen

coif – a close-fitting cap, often made of white linen or silk and decorated with lace

damask – a beautiful, self-patterned silk cloth woven in Flanders. It originally came from Damascus – hence the name

daybooke – a book in which you would record your sins each day so that you could pray about them. The idea of keeping a diary or journal grew out of this. Grace is using hers as a journal

doublet – a close-fitting padded jacket worn by men

farthingale – a bell - or barrel-shaped petticoat held out with hoops of whalebone

harbinger – somebody who went ahead to announce the monarch

jerkin – a close-fitting, hip-length, usually sleeveless jacket

kirtle – the skirt section of an Elizabethan dress

Lady-in-Waiting – one of the ladies who helped to look after the Queen and who kept her company

lime wash – a mixture of lemon and lime to lighten and strengthen the hair and make it shine

lockjaw – the old name for tetanus, owing to the fact that an inability to open the jaw was an early symptom of the infection

madrigals – beautiful part-songs which were very fashionable

Maid of Honour – a younger girl who helped to look after the Queen like a Lady-in-Waiting

manchet bread – white bread

Mary Shelton – one of Queen Elizabeth's Maids of Honour (a Maid of Honour of this name really did exist, see below). Most Maids of Honour were not officially 'ladies' (like Lady Grace) but they had to be of born of gentry

mazed – dazed, confused

mead – an alcoholic drink made with honey

Moor – a Muslim inhabitant of North Africa

mullioned glass – small pieces of glass held together by strips of lead to form a window

musk – a substance used in perfume which comes from a male musk deer

nosegay – a posy

Paris Garden – an area on the south bank of the Thames. It was said to be a pleasant walk, with inns for refreshment. It was adjacent to the area of the south bank famed for gambling and bear-baiting

partlet – a very fine embroidered false top, which covered just the shoulders and the upper chest

Paul's Chain – a street that led to St Paul's Churchyard. It is now known as 'Godliman Street'

pillion seat – a saddle for a woman which included a soft cushion

plague – a virulent disease which killed thousands

pomander – a mixture of aromatic herbs kept in a bag and used to fragrance clothes, or carried as a guard against infection

powder of alum – a combination of aluminium and potassium first used by the ancient Egyptians. In Elizabethan times it was used as a base in skin whiteners, and also as an underarm deodorant because it stopped the bacteria that make underarms smell

Presence Chamber – the room where Queen Elizabeth received people

Privy Chamber – the room where the Queen would

receive people in private

Privy Garden – Queen Elizabeth's private garden
on progress – term used when the Queen was
touring parts of her realm. It was a kind of summer
holiday for her

pursuivant – one who pursues someone else

Rood – a cross, often found in a church, representing
the cross on which Jesus was crucified

Secretary Cecil – William Cecil, an administrator for
the Queen (was later made Lord Burghley)

small beer – weak beer

Still Room – a room, usually near the kitchen, where
drinks, medicines and potions were prepared

sweetmeats – sweets

Tilting Yard – area where knights in armour would
joust or 'tilt' (i.e. ride at each other on horseback
with lances)

tinder box – small box containing some quick-
burning tinder, a piece of flint, a piece of steel and a
candle for making fire and thus light

tiring woman – a woman who helped a lady to dress

tumbler – acrobat

vellum – fine parchment made from animal skin

waterman – a man who rowed a ferry boat on the
Thames – he was a kind of Elizabethan cab driver

woodwild – crazy, mad

THE FACT BEHIND THE FICTION

In 1485 Queen Elizabeth I's grandfather, Henry Tudor, won the battle of Bosworth Field against Richard III and took the throne of England. He was known as Henry VII. He had two sons, Arthur and Henry. Arthur died while still a boy, so when Henry VII died in 1509, Elizabeth's father came to the throne and England got an eighth king called Henry – the notorious one who had six wives.

Wife number one – Catherine of Aragon – gave Henry one daughter called Mary (who was brought up as a Catholic), but no living sons. To Henry VIII this was a disaster, because nobody believed a queen could ever govern England. He needed a male heir.

Henry wanted to divorce Catherine so he could marry his pregnant mistress, Anne Boleyn. The Pope, the head of the Catholic Church, wouldn't allow him to annul his marriage, so Henry broke with the Catholic Church and set up the Protestant Church of England – or the Episcopal Church, as it's known in the USA.

Wife number two – Anne Boleyn – gave Henry another daughter, Elizabeth (who was brought up as a Protestant). When Anne then miscarried a baby boy, Henry decided he'd better get somebody new, so he accused Anne of infidelity and had her executed.

Wife number three – Jane Seymour – gave Henry a son called Edward, and died of childbed fever a couple of weeks later.

Wife number four – Anne of Cleves – had no children. It was a diplomatic marriage and Henry didn't fancy her, so she agreed to a divorce (wouldn't you?).

Wife number five – Catherine Howard – had no children either. Like Anne Boleyn, she was accused of infidelity and executed.

Wife number six – Catherine Parr – also had no children. She did manage to outlive Henry, though, but only by the skin of her teeth. Nice guy, eh?

Henry VIII died in 1547, and in accordance with the rules of primogeniture (whereby the first-born son inherits from his father), the person who succeeded him was the boy Edward. He became Edward VI. He was strongly Protestant, but died young in 1553.

Next came Catherine of Aragon's daughter, Mary, who became Mary I, known as Bloody Mary. She was strongly Catholic, married Philip II of Spain in a diplomatic match, but died childless five years later. She also burned a lot of Protestants for the good of their souls.

Finally, in 1558, Elizabeth came to the throne. She reigned until her death in 1603. She played the marriage game – that is, she kept a lot of important and influential men hanging on in hopes of marrying her – for a long time. At one time it looked as if she would marry her favourite, Robert Dudley, Earl of Leicester. She didn't though, and I think she probably never intended to get married – would you, if you'd had a dad like hers? So she never had any children.

She was an extraordinary and brilliant woman, and during her reign, England first started to become important as a world power. Sir Francis Drake sailed round the world – raiding the Spanish colonies of South America for loot as he went. And one of Elizabeth's favourite courtiers, Sir Walter Raleigh, tried to plant the first English colony in North America – at the site of Roanoke in 1585. It failed, but the idea stuck.

The Spanish King Philip II tried to conquer England in 1588. He sent a huge fleet of 150 ships, known as the Invincible Armada, to do it. It failed miserably – defeated by Drake at the head of the English fleet – and most of the ships were wrecked trying to sail home. There were many other great

Elizabethans, too – including William Shakespeare and Christopher Marlowe.

After her death, Elizabeth was succeeded by James VI of Scotland, who became James I of England and Scotland. He was almost the last eligible person available! He was the son of Mary Queen of Scots, who was Elizabeth's cousin, via Henry VIII's sister.

His son was Charles I – the King who was beheaded after losing the English Civil War.

The stories about Lady Grace Cavendish are set in the years 1569 and 1570, when Elizabeth was thirty-six and still playing the marriage game for all she was worth. The Ladies-in-Waiting and Maids of Honour at her Court weren't servants – they were companions and friends, supplied from upper-class families. Not all of them were officially 'ladies' – only those with titled husbands or fathers; in fact, many of them were unmarried younger daughters sent to Court to find themselves a nice rich lord to marry.

All the Lady Grace Mysteries are invented, but some of the characters in the stories are real people – Queen Elizabeth herself, of course, and Mrs Champernowne and Mary Shelton as well. There never was a Lady Grace Cavendish (as far as we know!) – but there were plenty of girls like her at Elizabeth's Court. The real Mary Shelton foolishly made fun of the Queen herself on one occasion – and got slapped in the face by Elizabeth for her trouble! But most of the time, the Queen seems to have been protective and kind to her Maids of Honour. She was very strict about boyfriends, though. There was one simple rule for boyfriends in those days: you couldn't have one. No boyfriends at all. You would get married to a person your parents chose for you and that was that. Of course, the girls often had other ideas!

Later on in her reign, the Queen had a full-scale secret service run by her great spymaster, Sir Francis Walsingham. His men, who hunted down priests and assassins, were called 'pursuivants'. There are also tantalizing hints that Elizabeth may have had her own personal sources of information – she certainly was very well informed, even when her counsellors tried to keep her in the dark. And who knows whom she might have recruited to find things out for her? There may even have been a Lady Grace Cavendish, after all!

A note on Elizabethan theatre

In 1576 Mr James Burbage opened the first permanent theatre, imaginatively called 'The Theatre'. It was a tall, round building and a single penny would get you inside to stand round the stage. It was noisy, smelly and crowded. A rich person would pay two pennies to have a seat in the galleries – or maybe even four pennies for a cushion! The rich were lucky because they got to sit. The poor would be standing for the whole of the play – sometimes three or four hours.

The Theatre was in Shoreditch, just outside the City of London. The Lord Mayor and his aldermen had decided that theatres were dreadful, sinful places, where diseases like the plague would spread, and they would not have one inside the city walls. This didn't stop people flocking to the theatre, though. One vicar actually complained that people preferred to watch a filthy play than come to church!

But in spite of the complaints, Queen Elizabeth loved watching plays, and during her reign play-going became increasingly popular. By the 1590s people were going to see plays by the most famous English playwright ever – William Shakespeare!

The stage didn't have any curtains to close, so

the playwright had to get his players off the stage in a way that seemed to be part of the play. If a character died, he either lay on stage until the end of the play, or he got carried off as part of the scene. After all, a 'dead' body couldn't get up and walk off on its own.

There wasn't much scenery to look at. A chair might be used to show that the scene was indoors, and a branch to indicate a forest. To help, signs were held up to describe the setting, and for those who couldn't read, a player would step forward and describe the scene in words.

Like the scenery, costumes were very simple. The audience would know that the man in riding boots must be a messenger, and that the one with a crown was a king. Mostly the actors wore their ordinary clothes – apart from the men who were playing women, of course. Women weren't allowed to act at all – that would have been far too shocking. Instead, a beardless young man would play the heroine and would wear a beautiful dress. In fact, Queen Elizabeth once famously gave away some of her old clothes to a group of players for use as costumes. This was quite a gift, as clothes were extremely expensive and valuable in Elizabethan times.

It's no wonder that plays were popular. With no

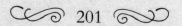

television, computers or films, the entertainment found at the theatre was most exciting. And the special effects were amazing! An actor might have an eye gouged out, and a nasty sticky mess would land on the stage. Actually, it was likely to be a squashed grape, but it would look very realistic. Someone might be stabbed so that their innards would spill out. Of course, it wouldn't really be their insides – someone would have been down to the butcher's shop for some animal entrails. One play famously ended with a battle scene and a real cannon was set off on stage. That made everyone shriek!

KEENE PUBLIC LIBRARY
60 Winter Street
Keene, NH 03431
352-0157